Books by Susan Traugh

Single Titles

The Edge of Brilliance

The Edge of Brilliance

ISBN # 978-1-78686-005-7

©Copyright Susan Traugh 2016

Cover Art by Posh Gosh ©Copyright 2016

Interior text design by Claire Siemaszkiewicz

Finch Books

Published in 2016 by Finch Books, Newland House, The Point, Weaver Road, Lincoln, LN6 3QN, United Kingdom.

THE EDGE OF BRILLIANCE

SUSAN TRAUGH

Dedication

To my daughters — and all young people who fight the demon of mental illness — and the caregivers who support them in that fight.

Prologue

"True heroism consists in being superior to the ills of life, in whatever shape they may challenge us to combat."
— Napoleon Bonaparte

"Dance with me, Mama." Fifteen-year-old Amy Miles stood eye to eye with her mother, arms extended wide, her expression full of hope and expectation. It didn't matter that her mother's arms were full of dirty dishes. It didn't matter that her mother was hot and disheveled from running around, cleaning the house. Amy caught her mother's eye looking past her, staring at the messy kitchen counter there beyond Amy's lithe, tan body, but Amy stood firm, smiling…asking…waiting for her mother's surrender.

And surrender she did.

With a lilting laugh, Amy slipped her arm around her mother's waist and, in cheek-to-cheek exuberance, dove into her mother's soft, spongy embrace as soon as the dishes touched the table. Barefoot, on tiptoe, they twirled and swooped in a modified waltz to the unheard music wafting through Amy's head.

Amy relished the smell of her mother's sweet sweat and jasmine lotion. She felt the older woman's breath warm against her nose, knowing that, in turn, her mother was delighting in the scent of her daughter as Amy's sure, strong muscles guided their steps around the living room carpet in the ballroom of Amy's imagination.

From the corner of her eye, Amy saw her mother's eyebrow furl in that look of consternation she always got when she was thinking of it all. But it didn't matter. Her mother's mind might seek to dwell in pain—Amy could only dance. The moment of pleasure pulsated in her and her only response was to let it guide her feet. Soft snatches of a tune escaped from Amy's throat as she took another spin around the carpet before planting the gentlest kiss on the woman's cheek and playfully fluttering butterfly kisses with her eyelashes. Mom's quiet chuckle let Amy know she'd successfully rescued her mother from that dark place and sent a ripple of satisfied giggles through Amy as she twirled her mother across the floor.

"Your skin feels so soft, Mama," Amy whispered as she felt her mother again fall into the kaleidoscope of her fears. They circled the floor once more in their one-two-three glide as snippets of Amy's inner tune lighted on the air in snatches of a hum. But her mother was far away.

A furrow formed on Amy's forehead and mock pain teased the edges of her playful voice. "This is where you say, 'Oh, thank you, daughter, for your nice compliment,'" Amy scolded her mom as she turned her lips into the woman's crêpe-draped neck and blew a tiny raspberry.

A laugh bubbled up Mom's throat as Amy uttered those words and snapped the older woman out of her sorrow.

"You're right!" Her mother laughed, kissing Amy's cheek. "Thank you, dear, sweet daughter, for your nice compliment—and our dance."

"You're welcome, my dear mother," Amy replied with a sparkle in her eye and drama flaring from her fingertips. Then, in her best Fred Astaire style, Amy pushed her back, twirled her mother under her arm and laid the disheveled woman into a most dramatic final dip.

Amy pulled her mother upright to soft laughter, planted a loud, sloppy kiss on her cheek and wordlessly walked away even as she saw the tears flowing down the woman's face.

Chapter One

Her wail reverberated off the tiled walls in a satisfying shriek. Drenched, enraged and prostrate, Amy reached her arms over her head as she lay fully clothed, sprawling half in, half out of the shower while steam roiled and the water splashed out of the open door and onto the floor.

"Manic," her dad had said. As if it was *his* word. As if he had any right to it. Any right to use it. It was hers. *Her* word. *Her* nightmare. *Her* disease.

Everyone tried to make this mess more manageable with cheery advice and condescending platitudes. But it was a curse. A plague. A full-blown disaster. She didn't deserve it and she'd wail at the wall if she wanted to.

Her therapist had once congratulated her on choosing the shower. He'd suggested cold water to cool her down and ease her manic episodes, so Amy purposely chose hot. Besides, the hot water mirrored her mood.

And yet, as the heat poured over her body, that rage seemed to seep out of her pores and flow down the drain with her tears. It was ending. She could feel the signs. But it was never raw rage into sublime peace. This trip to hell included a side trip through mortification and shame with a final destination of nothingness. And here it came again. After the volcano came the pit. Amy tried to hold on to her rage. As acidic as that fire burned, it was better than falling into the hole of despair that awaited her. For this was not the first time she'd locked herself away in fury. She just wanted it to be the last.

The rattle of the bathroom doorknob jolted Amy's thoughts as her mother successfully forced the locked door with the back of a spoon…again.

"Get out!" Amy shrieked, mustering all the anger she could pull from her waterlogged body before her mother opened the bathroom door. But she knew her mother had heard the change in her cries. They'd danced this dance so often that Amy knew her mother could anticipate each step, and the truth was, part of her was glad for her mom to come and pull her back from the volcano's pit.

"No," said her mother in a tone that allowed no response. Mom slowly closed the door behind her and surveyed the damage. She sucked in a quick breath, stopped, then slowly blew it out as if she were blowing through a straw. In her fury, Amy had slammed the shower door against the towel rack on the wall, shattering the tempered glass within the frame. The pebbles of glass hung in a weblike pattern on the door, glistening with the spray of the shower and looking like a thousand diamonds.

"He called me crazy!" Amy yelled from the shower floor, a new wave of rage enveloping her.

"I don't recall hearing him use that word," replied her mom.

"Manic, manic, manic!"

"Well, Amy, I'd say the shower door and living room furniture would attest to a manic episode…"

"But he can't *say* it!"

"What can he say, honey? What can any of us say when you're like this?"

Amy threw the soap at the shower wall. "But don't you get it? I don't *want* to be like this!"

"I understand that. But you will be until you start taking your meds regularly."

"I'm not crazy! I'm not taking meds for crazy people!"

"No one said you were crazy. Your father never used that word and never will. But you do have bipolar disorder. So your choice is to control your condition, or let the condition control you. We both know the choice you're making now. How's that working for you?"

While Amy wept, her mother stood staring at the wall. The steady pounding of the shower's water was the only other sound in the room. As she cried, Amy wondered if her mother would ever speak again.

"Who are you, Amy?" her mom asked.

Amy's words tumbled out as limp and water-laden as she was. "Your piece o' crap, screwed-up daughter. Isn't that what you want me to say?" And, despite herself, a new flood of angst escaped Amy's throat. Not rage, but shame, pain and aching need raced out from her soul and echoed around the shower floor. Once released, her sobs seemed to have no limits. *How could I do this again? Why couldn't I just control myself? Everybody else seems to be able to get a grip — why am I such a freak-girl? People are actually afraid of me! Afraid of me! If they could only see me now, sobbing in the shower, slobbering down my cheek. Only the constant stream of water washes my river of snot away. Oh God, what a hot mess I am. What a piece o' crap, hot mess.*

"No, that's definitely not what I want from you," replied Mom, as if she had heard Amy's thoughts. "I want a hopeful, dream-filled answer that will define your goals and pull your life forward. I don't know how to help you find it, but it's certainly not this way."

Amy had no other answer and simply lay crying in the shower. The water had washed away all her rage. The mania was ending and depression's grip was squeezing her throat. Amy knew her mom would help her. But she didn't know why she — or anyone — should, as that voice of shame wrapped its bony fingers around her skull, taunting her, teasing her. *You're such a screw-up. You're a burden on the family. Just disappear, asshole, and never burden your family again. Really. You know you understand why bipolar kids kill themselves. Wouldn't that peace be nice? It would just be so much easier… Life would be so much easier if…*

Deflated and empty, Amy had nothing left. She would have told her mother this fight was not done if she'd had the energy. She would have told her mom 'thank you' for coming to her rescue. But she couldn't open her mouth to say it. She couldn't say anything.

Mom reached up and turned off the water. She dropped a towel over the back of Amy's shoulders. "Come on, get up," she said as she slowly pulled her daughter to her feet. "Be careful not to touch the shower door or it might break all over you."

Wordlessly, she began to dry Amy's hair and face. Like a child, Amy sat on the toilet seat while her mom removed her shoes and socks then helped her discard her pants and shirt behind her towel-shield.

Amy walked out of the bathroom and toward her room in a zombie-like trance. As she passed, she glanced at the living room. Throw pillows were strewn all over the floor. The plaid easy chair was turned on its side and the flower arrangement sprinkled like confetti all over the rug.

"*Clean it up,*" her mother had said as the manic had begun. But Amy had only been able to destroy then. Now she could barely walk.

She stumbled into her room and fell onto her bed. Only when she had already lain down did she realize that her light was still on. Too tired to do anything about it, she simply threw her arm over her eyes and fell asleep.

* * * *

As the morning sun shone on her face, the first thing Amy felt was that gnawing feeling in the pit of her stomach telling her something was wrong. Before she even opened her eyes, she knew she didn't want to pinpoint the source of that feeling.

Stupid. Stupid. But there it was. She couldn't even forget for a second. The whole ugly scene spread out in digital clarity right there under her closed eyelids. *Stupid. Crazy. Out of control.* How humiliating. And now she had to walk downstairs and look them in the eye. She pulled the covers over her head. Couldn't she just stay under the covers and die? Couldn't she just disappear and never come back? Truth was, her folks would probably be happy if she were gone. No more crazy girl. No more drama queen. Oh God, did she really break the shower door? "Just shoot me and put me out of my misery," she mumbled under her breath.

"Get up, Amy, you gotta go to school," Lizzie called into her room.

"Leave me alone, I don't feel good," Amy snarled.

"Well, duh! After your little episode last night? I should guess not."

"It's not my fault."

"Well, actually, it is. You don't see me throwing tizzy-fits anymore. Thought about taking your meds?"

"You don't understand. You don't have it as bad as me…"

"Oh, puh-leese. Cut me a break. Don't play victim with me. That shower door just cost us all the trip to Disneyland. So, thank you very much. As I see it, *you* have no reason to whine." Lizzie turned and walked out of the door, then popped her head back in for a parting shot. "Just take your damn meds."

Amy hated it when Liz did that turn-on-your-heel crap that always stopped the argument. It made Amy feel as if she'd lost. And she hated to lose an argument. *Disneyland. Damn. Why can't life go back to how it was?* She'd once been the star. An A student. A dancer. She had even been class president. Everything had been so easy then. She'd even been happy. Really. Happy. Then puberty came and with it bipolar disorder. Amy couldn't remember a happy day since. It wasn't fair. It wasn't her fault she had manic episodes. Why should she be punished? Dad had the bad gene pool. Of course, Mom's genes weren't that great either. Amy was doomed by DNA beyond her control. Pills. That was Lizzie, of course. Pop a pill and life would be okay. Better living through chemistry. Well, Amy had her own chemistry.

Amy got up and started slamming around her room. She reached for her T-shirt, but it wouldn't come out of the drawer. She jerked the shirt hard and the drawer flew open. Amy shoved it back and it crashed into the dresser, knocking over her bottle of Juicy perfume. Like dominoes, the perfume hit the cat figurine she'd painted at Coffee and Clay and chipped its chin. In anger, Amy spun away from the dresser and kicked her shoe across the room, where it bounced off the wall, leaving a black mark. It was going to be another rotten day.

Sullenly, she went downstairs and sat at the table. She poured herself a bowl of cereal, hoping that her mother would just let her eat in silence.

"How are you today, Amy?"

No such luck. She was going to have to talk.

"Fine."

"Don't forget you have dance practice after school today, and here's a check to replenish your lunch account." Mom always began with business as usual. She started to reach out for Amy's hunched shoulders. Amy could see her mom poised above her through her hair, but she didn't move. Mom's hand fluttered above Amy's arm, hesitated and pulled back.

"Mommy, can I get a check for lunch money? I'm out," Lizzie said as she darted from cupboard to cupboard looking for something for breakfast.

"Sure, baby. Just bring me my checkbook. I didn't know you were out of money, too."

Opposite of Amy in every way, Lizzie relished being her mother's 'baby' and, despite a stack of college applications as high as her head, was in no hurry to grow up. Or at least in the way Amy wanted to grow up.

"Thanks, Mommy," chirped Lizzie. "Here you go," she said, handing her mother her satchel from beside the door.

As Mom began to write out the check, she turned back to Amy, carrying on in the same matter-of-fact manner.

"Do you need me to pick you up today or are you still going to Stacey's?" Dr. David had said that Amy's manics weren't punishable offenses. "You can't punish someone well," he'd instructed. Dr. David had pointed out that Amy's withdrawn behavior demonstrated her humiliation at her so-called 'episodes'. Mom's job, he said, was to help her find the tools to stop a manic before it started, or, failing that, to recover from it as quickly as possible.

"No."

"No, what? You don't need me to pick you up or you're not going to Stacey's?"

"Mom! I don't know. I'll call you. Okay?"

"Careful," said Mom.

"Sorry."

Her mom stood up and kissed Amy on the top of the head, then headed to the back of the house. Amy put her bowl in the sink, grabbed her books and went off to school.

* * * *

Stacey was waiting the second Amy got off the bus.

"Giiirrrlll—get over here!" Stacey's voice was playful as she grabbed Amy's arm. "Jeff just talked to me. He came right up to the pole and leaned on the other side! I'm telling you— Hey, what's with you? Why didn't you straighten your hair? You sick? You look wrecked."

"I'm fine," said Amy as she turned and sauntered back behind building B, taking the long way to humanities. Stacey followed at the same slow pace, walking beside her friend in total silence.

"Whatever," Stacey said, as if the conversation had never lulled. "We're late for class—again. Let's go in the back door."

Pulled from that silent place, Amy followed Stacey to the classroom. Stacey and Amy slipped in the back and quietly scooted into the back two chairs.

"Nice of you to join us, ladies," said Mr. Cooper, "but don't even think of sitting next to each other. Stacey, up here." Mr. Cooper pointed at the empty chair in the front row.

Stacey smiled and winked at Amy before strolling to the front of the room. Tall and lean, with her copper-colored hair and copper eyes, Stacey was easy to spot in any room, but now she walked up the aisle in her best supermodel stride. In fact, she had been taking classes to try to pursue a modeling career, and if that catwalk was any example, she was clearly ready for the big time. And her sultry saunter was not ignored by any of the males in the classroom — not even Mr. Cooper, although he tried to hide his interest with a feigned look of irritation.

"Why, thank you, Mr. Cooper," Stacey cooed, dramatically seating herself as the class twittered into their books.

"As I was saying…" Without missing a beat, Mr. Cooper continued to drone on about the ancient Sumerians. With his slight build and big, dorky glasses, Amy thought he resembled one of those drone bees always hovering just outside the nest. Buzzing, annoying, but never quite fitting in. And speaking of buzzing, the man just loved to hear his own voice. Now science — that was a class. Everything was group projects and experiments. But not Cooper. Cooper was all about words, words, words. "And, class, don't forget about your report. I'll expect you to be able to read your thesis next class." Blah. Blah. Blah. Amy was just about to doze off when the bell rang.

Amy and Stacey shot out of the room. Pushing shoulder to shoulder, they negotiated past the crowds filling the hallway and managed to get ahead of the pack. Their timing was perfect, and they met Kairyn just as she was coming out of English.

"So, we decided," Stacey jumped in before Kairyn had even noticed her friends. "We decided that our costumes are too bland."

"What are you talking about?" Kairyn turned at the sound of Stacey's voice.

"Everyone is going to have leotards and skirts," Amy began. The energy of the hallway had begun to revive her from Cooper's anesthesia and her manic malaise. "What if we went techno and filled our arms with bracelets? I got the beads the other day. We can all come to my house and have a candy party."

"Sounds great!" said Kairyn. "'You got enough for everyone?"

"Probably. Maybe. Who knows? Let's just string until they're gone and find out. After dance?"

"Cool," said Kairyn as she turned back to head to Mr. Cooper's room.

"Later," chimed Stacey and Amy as they headed off to English.

"So what'd you do to get Jeff to talk to you?" Amy winked. "A little tease?"

Stacey hit Amy in the arm. "Gross. Stop. No, really. He just wanted to know if we were going to the beach this weekend. Let's go, okay? God, Amy, he's so cute."

"Yeah, let's go. It'll be fun. Did you see my new gold bikini?"

"No, did your mom let you get it?"

"Yeah, but she may change her mind."

"Really? Why?"

"No reason. You know how she is."

"Yeah, well, there's the bell. Bye."

"Bye."

After school, the girls raced into dance. Everyone loved dance, but it was Amy's sanctuary. The flow of energy through her trunk and into her elongated arms and legs felt like ecstasy to her. Amy's body just knew how to move. She didn't have to think. She didn't have to listen to the teacher or concentrate. It was as if each muscle and tendon knew the dance before the teacher ever began. Ms. Grayson would make a move and Amy's body could answer before the set was finished. If only the rest of her life could work so flawlessly.

"Five, six, seven, eight…" Ms. Grayson pulled Amy from her dreaming. "Step ball change, step ball change, plié, step, plié, drop, three and four, roll, roll, seven and freeze.

Again."

Amy didn't need to do it again. Her body knew every move, but the others were struggling with the set. Amy stood up and flowed in complete harmony with the universe.

While they practiced, one by one the rest of the troupe caught up to Amy. As they did, her eyes tracked the flow of arms in unison, the wave of bodies dipping and lunging in perfect time, the colorful flash of myriad leotards leaping and dropping as one. She breathed in the smell of women and sweat and jazz shoes. In her bones she absorbed the sounds of the music, the beat of their steps on the wooden floor and the soft feminine pants of hard work. Lost in her joy, before Amy knew it, the hour was gone and it was time to go home. Back to her mom. Back to the scene of her latest destruction. Back to her misery.

* * * *

Dear Diary,

So, I manic-ed again. Shit. I didn't tell Stacey because she thinks it's funny to call me 'crazy girl'. I really hate that. The truth is, I'm afraid she's right. I sometimes look at Ray when he's collecting cans from the dumpster outside Taco Heaven and wonder – could that be me? You know they say that most homeless people are crazy.

Why do I keep doing this? I'll be fine. I'll just know I have it under control – just know. And then it hits me again. I work so hard, so hard, to keep things under control. I know other people don't have to work this hard. Yet I fail…every time.

But maybe it wasn't my fault this time. Yeah, I was pissed, but Dad called me 'manic'. He knows I hate that word and he said it anyway. If he hadn't said it, I bet I wouldn't have flipped out. He's just got to learn to not call names. Anybody would get pissed if they got called a name like that. Not just me.

I'm not even sure you could call it a 'manic'. Yeah, I broke the shower door – damn, can you believe Mom canceled Disneyland because of that? I can't believe she'd act like that. If the towel rack wasn't right there, it never would have happened. Anyway, it could have happened to anyone. You didn't even have to be mad – just open the door too hard. It really wasn't my fault and now look. It just feels so unfair. I hate my life.

Amy

Chapter Two

Amy walked in the house with Stacey and Kairyn. Friends were always a good offense. Mom would never start a post-manic lecture in front of anybody.

"Grab some snacks!" Amy yelled to Stacey.

Stacey had long ago lost her guest status in the house. In fact, since Amy was always ordering Stacey around the kitchen, Stacey actually knew where stuff was better than Amy herself. Stacey grabbed some chips and apples, then found a couple of cans of soda and headed upstairs.

In her room, Amy began pulling out the beads as Kairyn sprawled on the bed. "So, spill about Jeff…"

"Jeff?" Kairyn shot a shocked look over to Stacey. "Oh my God, you hooked up with Jeff?"

"No, no, no!" Stacey laughed, but her face glowed red. "It's not like that. He just talked to me, that's all. But he *talked* to me. I'm so excited. Do you know how cute he is?"

"Those black eyes…" Amy began.

"And his hair that waves just like this over his eye…" Kairyn's hand waved over her eye in an exaggerated expression of Jeff's hair.

"And he's even got a six-pack…"

"Nuh-uh."

"Well, kinda…"

"So, what about you?" teased Kairyn, nodding toward Amy. "You seen J-J lately?"

"That's done."

"No way," chimed in Stacey. "I know you still like him. What's up?"

"Nothing."

"My ass."

"Your ass is right," said Amy. "He cheated. I know, you said he would. But I really thought he'd changed."

"Once an ass, always an ass."

"But I liked him."

"So, should I start a rumor that he's gay?" asked Stacey.

"Good and loyal friend," Amy exclaimed with a queenly sweep of her arm, "be my guest — although I doubt anybody would believe you."

"Probably not...but it would be fun to see how far it'd get."

Everyone laughed as they beaded and snacked throughout the afternoon. Amy was struck by the beauty of her friends, sprawled across the bed as they beaded, shifting from one intertwined tableau to another with arms and legs carelessly thrown over each other, stringing together beads and stringing together stories. *If only I could freeze the good moments*, she thought. *If only I could hold on to this peace.*

"Cynthia asked how you were," Stacey offered.

"Who cares?" Amy scowled.

"Well, you — "

"Don't."

"Are you ever gonna forgive her?"

"No."

"That seems unfair, Amy."

"She ditched me."

"No, her mom *made* her ditch you."

"I can't be your friend, Amy." Amy's whiny mimic made both girls snicker. "My mom says your behavior is inappropriate."

"But, you know her mom..." Kairyn offered.

"No excuse." Amy tossed her bracelet onto the bed and strode across the room to rearrange her desk. "She thinks she's getting into some fancy college 'cause she wants to be a rocket scientist and so she can't hang around crazy girls. Who wants to be a rocket scientist, anyway? Besides, when I'm a famous dancer, she'll be sorry. She'll come back with her dorky degree and want to be cool and see me in some Broadway show. She'll say, 'Hey, Amy, remember me? Can you get me tickets?' and I'll say 'Who the hell are you? I only remember friends. I only remember people who stayed by me and understood...' – like you two!" And with that, Amy ran across the room and jumped on the bed, knocking beads everywhere.

"Amy! Are you nuts? Look what you've done!" Stacey yelled as she rolled over and wrestled Amy off the bed.

"Don't call me nuts!"

"Then don't act stupid! You messed up my bracelet."

"Tough!"

"Tough back!" laughed Stacy as she pinned Amy to the floor.

"Amy, would you grow up! We're not children. Get up and let's finish our work!" Kairyn stood over the two panting friends.

"Sure," replied Stacey as she grabbed a handful of chips and threw them at Kairyn.

"Oh, please, you're just as bad..." Kairyn turned and began to pick up beads as Amy continued to laugh and struggle under Stacey's giggling grip.

Just then Mom called the girls down to dinner. The game was quickly forgotten as the smell of Italian food wafted up the stairs. Lizzie was staying late for drama rehearsal, and with Dad still at work, the friends had the table to themselves. Amy stuck a piece of garlic bread in her mouth before passing the basket to Stacey. Kairyn pulled a big scoop of steaming spaghetti from the bowl, splashing red sauce all over the front of her white T-shirt as she plopped it onto her plate.

"Slob," teased Amy.

"Pig," retorted Kairyn, motioning to Amy's bread-stuffed mouth.

"It's good. Can't help it."

"I know, and I'm famished." And just to prove her point, Kairyn sucked up long strands of spaghetti with her loudest, juiciest slurping noises as the other two snorted.

"Glad you're hungry," Mom said as she poured milk for each of the girls. "After dinner, I'm taking you both home. Amy's got to get to bed early tonight."

Damn, Amy thought. The night had been going well. She'd thought her mom might just let the day pass without 'the talk', but it wasn't going to happen. 'Bed early' was code for 'no such luck, kid' and as soon as her friends were safely delivered home, Mom would be ready for a little sit-down. Would it ever end?

* * * *

The vibration from Stacey leaving and slamming the car door had not even shimmied across the car when Mom started.

"Did you think you could hide behind your friends forever?"

"I thought it was worth a shot."

"Don't get smart with me, young lady…"

"Then don't set me up with ridiculous questions."

"Enough. Have you any idea what this latest episode has cost this family?"

"I thought I wasn't supposed to be punished for manics…"

"Manics? No. Lack of compliance that leads to manics? You betcha."

"How's that different, Mom? You want to answer me that? You know bipolar people hate taking drugs. It's, like, part of the disease. That's so stupid of you. Like saying that chemotherapy patients can be punished for throwing up."

"They are not close to the same thing."

"Yes, they are."

"No…they're not."

"Bipolars hate meds. Seriously, what's the problem?"

"The problem is you're not 'a bipolar', you're a gifted and talented girl who has incredible potential if you'd attend to your illness."

"I can't help that I'm sick."

"Amy, this is a problem with compliance. This is a problem of you living in denial, refusing to take your medication and then believing that you're not responsible for the destruction you cause when your mood explodes — either up or down. It doesn't matter. You think I don't know about the drugs? You think I don't know that you're probably stealing? Do you think I'm a total idiot? Where does the money come from? How do you afford whatever it is you're popping? We don't give you money. We don't give you the opportunity to make it so you don't get yourself in trouble. But you find the trouble anyway, don't you? Is it you stealing from my purse? Was it you who took the pain pills from the cupboard?"

"What—? What—? Now you're accusing your own daughter? How am I supposed to trust you when you don't trust me? I told you I wasn't stealing! I told you I wasn't doing drugs! I told you it wasn't me taking money out of your purse! What kind of a mom accuses her own child? How dare you talk to me that way!"

Amy reached for the car door handle to let herself out. Her mom slammed on the brakes.

"Don't you even think about it!" she yelled, hitting the child lock.

"You child-locked me? You child-locked me? And then you wonder why I don't respect you? How dare you treat me like a child! How dare you show such a lack of respect!"

"What about respect for us? How much does this family have to suffer because you don't want to take your meds? How much do we have to lose so that you can have damned 'self-determination'? Here's the bottom line, young lady — I don't give a damn what the law says or how old you are. So long as you live under my roof, I am the law. And I say you will take your meds. Every day. Every pill. I don't care if they upset your stomach. I don't care if they upset your fragile little psyche. I don't care. I don't care. I don't care. You are not the only member of this family and I'm up to here with everyone else tiptoeing on eggshells around you, or sacrificing and losing everything because you don't want to take care of your illness. Grow up. Knock off the denial and get with the program. Period. End of conversation."

* * * *

As Amy sat in Cooper's class the next day, her mind wandered back to last night's talk and this morning's WWF sequel.

She'd been furious when her mom had forced her to take her meds. In fact, Mom had stood there that morning and watched Amy swallow each pill. Like she was a baby. No, like she was a prisoner. Or some whacko patient in the loony bin. Who did she think she was? She'd said Amy's behavior affected the whole family. Did she have any idea how *their* behavior affected *her*? Now Lizzie was blaming her for the Disneyland trip. Mom said she wasn't punishing Amy, but what did she call drugging her? Amy would bet there had to be some law that said drugging your kid was child abuse. She decided to look it up on the Internet. She'd bet the cops would be on her side. Just say no. Didn't that apply to all kids, or did bipolar kids have no rights? The whole thing pissed Amy off. She just wished everyone would leave her alone.

"Amy." Mr. Cooper's voice intruded on Amy's thoughts. He took off his black-rimmed glasses, folded them and held them as he crossed his arms over his chest before beginning again. "I asked if you had your assignment ready? Could you read us your thesis?"

Oh, no! The paper! Amy had totally forgotten the paper. *How could I be so stupid?* It was her mom. All Amy had been able to think of was the lecture that was coming and she'd completely forgotten about the paper. *Crap.*

"I wasn't feeling well last night, Mr. Cooper." Amy hoped her facial expression was pitiful enough for ol' Coop to buy.

"Amy, you've had two weeks to do an outline..." He

wasn't biting.

"Oh, and I do have it." Amy quickly regrouped. "I just forgot to put it in my notebook because I was sort of out of it."

"Well, get back into it and show me your thesis tomorrow with a note from your folks verifying your illness."

"Okay." Amy looked down at her desk. What were the chances Cooper would forget that he asked for a note? He'd called her mom once before. He might do it again, he was like that. Then she'd be in a world of hurt. She couldn't ask her mom for a note, she'd be grounded. But Cooper knew Stacey's writing and goody-two-shoes Lizzie would never help her out. *Crap. Crap. Crap. Why does this always happen to me?*

Stacey bumped into Amy's desk, startling her and making her shoot from her daydream.

"Move it, girl. Class is over. Or haven't you been tortured long enough?"

"Can you believe Coop — asking for a freakin' note? Now what am I gonna do?"

"You're screwed, dude. That's all."

"Thanks a lot."

"You're welcome. But come on. I got an idea."

Amy followed on Stacey's heels as Stacey maneuvered through the crowd in the hallway. As she strode on her long, model legs, Stacy ran her hand through her hair, fluffing it and shaking it into a just-laid cover-girl look. Stacey was heading toward the science building, which happened to be in the opposite direction of the English class they were supposed to be moving toward.

"Yo, Tan." Stacey sidled around in front of the tall, shy junior.

"Hello, Stacey." Tan's eyes lit up like Christmas and Amy suddenly felt sorry to be part of the plot she knew was unfolding.

Stacy tossed her copper mane in the sunshine as she slowly lifted her impressive eyelashes to look Tan in the eyes. The boy was toast. "I haven't seen you around for a while. How funny to run into you now. How're things?"

"They're good, Stace. But I need to get to class." The torture in the kid's eyes was difficult for Amy to watch, but she knew why Stacey was here and, while she really needed that paper, she couldn't let Stace manipulate Tan on her behalf.

"We're all hangin' at Amy's house tonight. Gonna get pizza. Want to come? I have that new CD you said you wanted."

"By Bad Knife?"

"That'd be the one."

"You don't mind?" His eyes could not get any wider as he looked for Amy's approval.

"Oh, Tan, I'm sorry." Amy grabbed Stacey's arm to keep her quiet. "Stace didn't know that I'm grounded. Some other time, okay?" And with that, she pushed Stacey into the flow of students heading to class.

"What's going on, bitch? I was saving your ass," snapped Stacey.

"I know, and I appreciate it. I just couldn't screw Tan that way. He never did anything to me."

"Whatever, bitch."

"Yeah, whatever."

* * * *

Dear Diary,

I could've saved my ass with Stacey's plan to get Tan to do my paper, but I couldn't. Now I'm screwed. I just don't know why this happens all the time. I'll have my work under control then some assignment just jumps out of nowhere due tomorrow. I can't do the paper tonight. At least, not well. I'll have to fake it and hope Coop is too tired to read it. Yeah, fat chance. Well, welcome to my downward spiral. Let me just die.

Amy

Chapter Three

Although she would never say it to her mother, Amy had to admit that the meds were making her feel better. The pit of doom was not so deep. That edge of manic didn't feel like it sat so close. But there was something else, something she couldn't really pinpoint. Maybe it was kind of a relaxation. Like her body had just let out a big 'ahhh'.

She'd stopped fighting the drugs and her mom had stopped the daily med check. At least some things were getting better. But now she was sitting in the waiting room of Dr. David's and she was pissed.

The waiting room actually prepared clients for what lay ahead. White walls, faded Kmart prints and ten-month-old magazines with their covers torn off and the pages rubbed to a velvet texture—it was dull and boring. Once in his office, things got no better.

"So, how are things?" Dr. David's first question was nothing if not predictable.

"Fine."

"What's been going on?"

"Nothing."

"Did you tell your folks you've been smoking?"

"No."

"Did you tell them you've been smoking marijuana?"

"No."

"Did you tell them you're experimenting with other drugs?"

"No."

"Why not?"

"Why should I?" The rules were clear. Dr. David was not

allowed to tell anyone anything Amy said in therapy unless she was going to go out and commit a crime, hurt someone or off herself. Clearly, there was no reason to confess anything regardless of what he wanted.

"How are you doing on the meds?"

"Fine."

Dr. David sighed and sat quietly for a second. "Amy," he said, "we've been doing this for a while. Here's how it works. I ask questions and you start talking about what's going on. Or, if you don't like my questions, you tell me what you want or need to talk about. That way, together, we can help you obtain the tools you need to manage your life and your bipolar disorder a little better."

"There's nothing to talk about."

"Oh? Your mom called me about the shower door. Do you want to talk about that?"

"No."

"Because…"

"Because it's none of your business…"

"Well, that's where you're mistaken. It actually *is* my business. I spent a lot of years in college studying hard to make it my business. See those degrees on the wall? See that certificate declaring me a psychologist? They say it is exactly my business. So, you want to tell me what triggered that episode?"

A hot ball of rage began to grow and spin in her chest. Amy didn't know. It hurt her brain to even think about it. And it pissed her off that everyone wanted to talk about it. It was over. It was done. She wasn't going to Disneyland. She was a stupid, crazy person. *So drop it already and move on.*

"What are you thinking?"

"I'm thinking I don't want to talk about it."

"You seem agitated."

Amy felt her breath moving in and out of her chest. She could hear it in her ears. Yeah, she was agitated. She wanted to jump up off that old, faded couch and run her arm over the top of his desk, throwing all his crummy books and piles of messy papers onto the floor. She wanted to take that mug of tea and splash it into that bookcase groaning under the weight of a million books with such disgusting titles as *Quirky, Yes – Hopeless, No*, or *How to Relate to Your Brain-Injured Child*, or *The Difficult Child*. Instead, she picked at the thread that popped from the seam of the cushion.

They sat that way, in total silence, for what seemed like a century. Finally Amy couldn't stand it anymore.

"What?" she asked.

"What are you thinking?" Dr. David asked in that calm, quiet tone that infuriated Amy. She hated how he could just sit back, rubbing his fingers along the edge of her file, legs crossed, his face quiet as he pushed her buttons and purposely set her off.

"I'm thinking I hate it here. I'm thinking that I'm not crazy and I hate that everyone treats me like I am. I hate that I'm being punished for something that's out of my control and that it's just not fair."

"Okay, good, Amy. Let's discuss what you just said."

"Let's not."

"All right, then let me talk about what you just said. First of all, you're not crazy. I hate that word, but if we're going to use it, it really applies to people who are out there in the world behaving inappropriately and not doing anything about it. The truth is, we're all 'crazy' in one way or another. It's the sane ones – the caring and committed ones – who seek out therapy and do the hard work of controlling their, as you say, 'craziness'. In fact, I think the whole world could use a little therapy. It's just the smart ones, like you, who come to get the tools they need to cope."

Dr. David stood up and began to rummage through his file cabinet. Amy always imagined that he'd gotten the cabinet from some wizard's school. It was old and scratched and so smashed full of old photocopied papers that the drawers wouldn't even close. As he pawed through what substituted for files, he continued to talk.

"But you're not being punished. I told you, I told your mom — manics aren't punishable offenses any more than pneumonia or diabetes. You are responsible for your mess, and you need to clean it up. But you are not responsible for your illness."

He'd clearly found whatever he was looking for, as his face lit up and he turned around to drop a blank invoice form in Amy's lap.

"That said, you have to pay for the shower door. There's the form. Pay it back in hourly labor to your family. We talked about how to lessen the damage of a manic. Hit a pillow. Throw clothes. Don't smash flat screens. Don't throw cell phones. I didn't mention shower doors, but then, I'll admit, it never occurred to me that you could throw one of those. However, I should have remembered how creative you are."

Against her will, Amy had to smile. It was one of the things she hated about Dr. David — he could get to her even when she didn't want him to.

"So, Amy, what triggered you?"

"Dr. David, I don't know what triggered it and I don't care. But Mom is forcing me to take my meds. Like I'm some prisoner that needs to be drugged. Isn't that an invasion of privacy? How'd you like it if I forced you to swallow drugs against your will?"

"Why do you think she's checking on your compliance like that?"

"I don't know."

"I think you do."

"Because she wants to drug me into zombie-hood. I'm difficult and if she just dopes me up I'll be easier for her to handle."

"So, you don't think this has anything to do with what is best for you?"

"No."

"Why are you so opposed to meds?"

"*I'm not crazy!*"

29

"No, you certainly are not. But you are bipolar. Not medicated, you suffer wicked manic episodes that can alter your brain forever." He stood up to get a book with pictures of brain scans in it that Amy had seen a dozen times.

"Did you know that the more manics you have, the more difficult they are to control? Or that, uncontrolled, nearly twenty percent of bipolar people commit suicide?" He dropped the book into her lap, opened, again, to a brain scan she had practically memorized, he showed it to her so often.

"We caught your disorder early. With meds and therapy, you can live a full, rich life. You may need to take breaks occasionally when things get out of control, but those are minor inconveniences. The other option is a life totally out of control—which, by the way, seems to be your coping method at the moment. You wouldn't begrudge a diabetic his insulin, or a heart patient his heart medicine. Why is your medication any different?"

"It just is." Amy slammed the book shut, blocking the bright brain scans from her vision and adding a sharp period to the end of her sentence.

"And that's why we're here, Amy," he said, ignoring the slam of the book. "We need to help you find a way to make this okay with yourself. If you want to have any kind of a life, you have to come to grips with your illness and take your meds. Maybe think of yourself as the quintessential hero called to battle. You've been given a challenge—a hard one—and the weapons to battle the beast. Are you going to attempt the challenge, or are you going to run? For, Amy, this won't go away no matter how much you might wish it. You will need to take your meds and have a good therapist for the rest of your life. And the sooner you can accept that and just move on, the sooner you can start building a real life for yourself."

Amy knew the tears were right under her eyelids, but no way would she cry in front of Dr. David. So she concentrated on that thread in the sofa. She rolled it around between her thumb and forefinger. She felt its firm line skid across the pad of her thumb as she watched the sharp contrast of black thread against pale skin. She felt her breath shudder in her chest as she tried to calm herself and she focused on keeping her face as still and expressionless as possible. In infuriating silence he sat, motionless except for the slow turning of his pen. He would not read her face. He would not make her cry.

She sat in silence until the end of the session.

* * * *

Dear Diary,

I hate Dr. David! Why the hell do I have to go to therapy? Do I look like I need my head shrunk? It really pisses me off that everybody thinks I have to talk about everything all the time. Nobody else does. I'm no different from Stacey or Kairyn. You don't see their folks making them go to therapy. Teenagers are supposed to be difficult. You can read that anywhere. I'm just acting like a regular teenager and I get all medicated and shrunk. It sucks. Do you hear me? It sucks.

Amy

Chapter Four

They sat in the palm of her hand like miniature beads from a broken bracelet. The oblong white one controlled her anger. The small, round blue one stabilized her hormones. Next to it, the round white pill lowered her anxiety level while at the same time relieving her depression. The apricot-colored hexagonal pill was a mood stabilizer. And on and on.

Amy looked at the tiny pile of tiny pills rolling on her palm. Altogether they didn't take up a space the size of a dime.

How could such a little bit of matter matter so much? How could so little substance create such havoc in her life—both when she took it and when she didn't?

Her mom had decided again to try to trust Amy with self-administration of her meds. Stupid Mom. She thought appealing to Amy's maturity and integrity would force her to responsibly swallow this poison every day.

"They're a miracle," her mother had declared one day when she'd balked at her pills. "A hundred years ago they would have locked you in an asylum and thrown away the key. They'd have declared you possessed and burned you at the stake."

Way to make me feel good, Mom. Lumping her in with witches and loonies really wasn't the way to form alliances or encourage cooperation.

"Amy," her mom had lectured—again, "you live in a miraculous time when just a few little pills can give you your life back, can let you become all that you can be and control a disorder that before this moment, was uncontrollable and utterly devastating."

Amy had turned her back and rolled her eyes. If she had to hear one more 'The Miracle of Modern Medicine' speech, she'd puke.

"Better living through chemistry," her dad had joked.

But it wasn't a joke. Amy rotated her hand to the left and to the right. The pills bounced and rolled over one another like frolicking children. Yet there was no joy in the taking. They upset her stomach, causing a constant low-grade nausea that made her feel cranky and wishing she could puke. They made her feel like she was walking in cement so that all she really wanted to do was fall into a zombie state and sleep. They formed a veil over her brain so that when she'd finished reading an assignment, she had no recollection of what the words had said. True, they never let her get really down, but they never let her get really happy either. Great, if all you wanted to do was control your kid, but pure torture if you were the one getting drugged and thought you might be entitled to…what? Joy? Passion? Happiness? Maybe an occasional giggle-fest? No, it wasn't better living through chemistry — it was really no life at all.

Yet when she didn't take them, when she missed even a day or two, she'd have manics. She'd lose control of 'her' and become that other person. And that person did things. That person shoplifted. That person made out with scumbags. That person tore apart rooms, got in trouble with cops, told off best friends.

Or she crashed. No one knew how deep that pit was. No one knew how she'd tied the grocery bag over her face to end it all, or tried to cut her wrist before Stacey had snatched the knife, or grabbed the steering wheel to turn into traffic before the other guys in the car yelled at her and pulled back from the center divider. No one knew how ending it all was a thousand times better than this minute, or the next, or the next.

Maybe burning at the stake wasn't such a bad idea after all.

Amy closed her fingers while she walked over to the sofa. There she lifted the wooden arm panel to reveal a hollow space in the couch and dropped the pills into the hidden place next to the colorful supply already scattered beneath.

Chapter Five

Amy's body tingled with excitement. The dance recital was tomorrow and Amy felt like one of those old-fashioned jack-in-a-box toys. As dress rehearsal had begun, she'd felt wound up to an excruciating level and she now sat in the dark—taut, tense and ready to spring.

Their costumes were incredible, with black face masks, leotards and tights under white leggings, and white opera gloves covered with about a foot of beaded bracelets. At the crucial moment in the dance, the lights would go out, black lights would come on and the girls would appear to be floating arms and legs dancing in the dark. The mythical, ethereal quality of the floating body parts appealed to Amy.

As she practiced at the dress rehearsal, Amy envisioned the awe of the audience and how her performance would rehabilitate her reputation at school. She'd been the subject of an awful smear campaign of late. Kids were saying she was a druggie and a slut. It was all untrue. But it hurt nevertheless, so it was good that she'd get a chance to show her true self. Her name was even going to be in the program as the choreographer of the piece.

Amy Marie Miles – Choreographer.

Co-choreographer, actually—after all, Ms. Grayson had done a lot of the work. But Amy had really pitched in and had good ideas. Ms. Grayson had praised her repeatedly for her natural talent as a choreographer. It was the one thread that she could grab on to in her day to stop herself from drowning in the quicksand of school and depression. And yet even as she danced, even as her triumph lay so near, the tingle of excitement began to turn. She felt the tug at her feet. The pit was near. The drag was getting stronger. No matter how much she worked, or danced, or concentrated, the pull into the pit was growing.

"Where'd you go, Amy?" Ms. Grayson's voice pulled Amy back to class.

"What?"

"Stephanie wondered if you had any extra white jazz shoes. You're the same size and she doesn't have any. You did decide on white, right?"

"Oh yeah."

"Yeah, what?"

"Yeah, we did decide on white so our feet would show up under the black lights. And, yeah, I have an extra pair you can borrow, Steph."

"Thanks."

"No problem."

"Then that's it," continued Ms. Grayson. "We'll have time to stretch, but no real warm-up tomorrow. So, practice tonight, girls... And get plenty of sleep. I mean it!"

The class began to break up as girls started moving toward the locker room to change.

"Hey, brat, I'm coming over." Kairyn had pushed into Amy and began handing her shoes, tights and gloves in an attempt to physically engage Amy.

"No, Kairyn, not tonight," Amy said, searching the room and handing Kairyn back her clothes.

"Don't do it." Kairyn reached for Amy's arm.

"What?" Amy continued to look past Kairyn as she slipped out of Kairyn's grasp.

"You know exactly what. Don't, I said. Really. It messes with your mind."

Amy stopped for a moment and, finally, looked at Kairyn's worried face. "My mind's already messed with," Amy said as she dropped her head and moved away from Kairyn.

"It doesn't do what you think. It doesn't really help." Kairyn tried to maneuver closer to Amy again, but Amy's eyes had spotted what she was searching for and she began to walk away from Kairyn as she threw a last remark over her shoulder.

"I don't know what you're talking about."

And with that, Amy turned her back to her friend and walked over to Stacey. "Hey, girl. What's up?"

Stacey smiled at Amy then dropped her head as the two girls shoved their costumes into plastic grocery bags. As Stacey tied up her bag she turned to Amy. "You in?"

"Yeah. Where?"

"The park."

"When?"

"Now."

"I'll go with you."

"No, just meet me there."

"Later."

"Later."

Amy walked out of the door and headed to the park. Reaching in her purse as she walked, she turned off her cell phone and dropped it back in its pouch. Then she turned the block before the park and made her way around the back route. If anyone was watching, it would look like she was heading over to Cynthia's house—not that she would ever go to Cynthia's. But if anyone asked, her alibi was set.

The tautness from class had returned. Amy's breath came as quickly as her steps and her heart was beating in her ears. *Tick. Tick. Tick. Tick.* The spring wound tighter and tighter in her chest. Her feet were off the ground. Her breath was pink vapor as light became liquid and sound splashed out in vivid color. *It's coming. It's coming.* Her steps began to quicken. *Tick. Tick. Tick. Tick. Salvation time is near. Tick. Tick. Tick. Tick. It's coming. It's coming. Tick. Tick. Tick. Tick. Escape from life is here.*

X. Beautiful, wonderful ecstasy. She already felt it coursing through her veins as she saw the first trees of the park. *Ah, love. Ah, sweet, blissful release. There you are. There you wait.* Just steps away. *Click. Click. Click. Click.* The heels of her shoes tapped out the rhythm of hope. Hope that she'd thought would elude her the rest of her life. Hope for love. Hope for escape. Hope for a few moments of real, true happiness. Amy knew the pit of another debilitating depression was licking at her heels, right on the other side of this building manic. If she could just get to the park first... *Tick. Tick. Tick. Tick.* The tautness twisted in her chest tighter and tighter as she measured her steps to the green grass of freedom. She couldn't run. She couldn't draw attention to herself. But... Beautiful, beautiful ecstasy was there, within reach, and with it hope and release and joy.

She saw J-J first. He simply lifted his head in acknowledgment then stepped back into the shadows around the bushes. Amy slipped into the sanctuary of green with J-J, Stacey and two other guys, neither of whom she'd ever seen. Stacey slipped some money into J-J's hand and turned to Amy.

"Gotta go, girl," she said. "My mom's tightened the leash and I gotta get home. Call me." She hurried toward the edge of the park. Everyone stood around quietly as Stacey walked away.

When she was out of sight, J-J held out his hand for cash.

Amy stopped cold. "Whadyamean?" she asked.

"No more freebies." J-J's voice was flat.

"But—"

"Free ride's over, kid." J-J never even raised his head to look at Amy as his words fell like stones.

Amy's breath came fast and shallow. She'd been rolling for a while. She wanted her X. She needed her X. It did everything her meds never did. It made her feel good, loved, happy, amazing, good...no, good. Didn't he get it? It was the only time she did feel good. Now no? What the—?

"You can't—" Amy could feel her rage rising red. She wanted to grab the bag. She wanted to claw his face. First he slept with that slut when he'd said they were a couple. Now this? Would he ever stop betraying her? Yet there everyone stood, smugly staring at her. "So, what?" She spat the words as she wanted to spit her contempt.

"You always have something of value." The smirk on J-J's face dripped, oozing acid down her spine.

"Bastard!" Amy turned to run away. She was going to cry. She was going to freak out right there in front of all these losers, and no way she'd give them the satisfaction. She'd turned and begun to follow Stacey's exit path when one of the new guys grabbed her arm while his buddy stepped into her way.

"May as well play nice," he said. "At least then you'll get your X." The smile on his face made her skin crawl.

"I don't want it that bad," she fairly snarled back.

"Yeah, but you need it," he sneered.

"Do not," Amy replied, but even she could hear the edge of fear in her voice.

"Yeah, you do. Look at you."

"X is not addictive." Red flags were flying all over her brain, but she couldn't leave. She couldn't let these lowlife creeps win. They had a deal. They were reneging and it just wasn't fair. She wasn't sure if her last comment was for them or herself, but the warning signals were flashing furiously in her brain.

"Maybe not for us. But you're you. Lil' manic girl. You need your little happy pills…"

"Piss off."

"Come on, bitch." His tone was getting menacing now. "Everybody knows you're a trout. So lay down and flop."

"Everybody may 'know' whatever they know. But I don't do that. I never have."

"Right." He laughed, clearly unimpressed by the truth.

"It's true. I'm no slut. I don't care what you've heard." Amy felt the lump rising in her throat. She hated when people called her names—especially when they weren't true.

"Maybe not. But you're gonna do me." He moved in just a little closer and stood up just a little taller. Amy smelled the cigarettes on his breath and the sweat of the day on his shirt.

"Am not — prick."

"Are so. Just decide how. Rough or easy. Your choice."
The finality in his voice sent a shiver up Amy's spine.

She looked at J-J for help. He'd once said he'd liked her.
She'd always thought he'd come back. She liked him. No,
she adored him. Yet he did this. He'd set this up. And now,
as her eyes pleaded, he just shrugged his shoulder.

"You're kidding. Right?" Amy's eyes begged J-J as her
voice rose half an octave. "Please."

"Of course. It's okay, kid. Here, I was just kidding…" And
J-J reached out and opened his hand to a beautiful pink pill
just waiting for her. "Here, take it."

Relief rushed over Amy as she swallowed the pill, and
when he opened his arms, Amy had no choice but to fall
into the safety of his embrace.

Amy's tension instantly fell away. J-J was just kidding.
He'd keep a handle on creep-boy here. She was just nervous
about the dance coming up and everything. She'd blown
the whole scene out of proportion. These guys weren't
trouble, just a little crude.

As he pulled her close, J-J's kisses were sweet and warm.
Amy savored the unexpected tenderness as he held her and
they talked together. Soon the other guys joined them in
conversation as J-J tenderly caressed her. *Oh my gosh, he's
back. He does love me after all.*

As she kissed J-J, she envisioned how she would arrive
at school tomorrow in triumph, J-J on her arm. Everyone
would see that she was special — she'd be J-J's girl, she'd be
amazing in her dance and her name would be featured in
the program.

As they continued to make out, J-J's hands became more
insistent, his kisses more passionate and his body more
immobilizing. But by then the ecstasy was kicking in.
Amy was so filled with love that her body exploded with
goodwill. She adored everything around her. She relished
the sensations as her senses peaked. J-J's scent turned to

liquid perfume trailing into her nostrils and undulating around her brain and through her veins. Each tree's green grew more vibrant as the kaleidoscope of the sun shot flashes of electric light through the branches to emblazon Amy's skin. She tasted the air. She directed the breeze. The smell of the grass was exotic intoxication. The sensation of fingers, tongues, hands on her body was…oh yes…it was pure, well, ecstasy. Amy loved J-J with every fiber of her being. And he loved her back. As the myriad intense sensations of the X saturated her senses, Amy fell into the pool of joy and happiness and relief that the drug offered her tortured mind, so that she hardly noticed when she was slowly pushed to the ground, pinned down and her legs forced open as she was passed from one demanding body, to another, and another.

Chapter Six

As Amy lay nestled within her bed, it seemed like the dream would never end. And yet it wasn't really a dream, but a memory of a different time. Only, it was as real as if she were there again. Amy was back in middle school. Stacey was there and they were in music together.

"Solo number four — goes to Amy!" She'd just known, back then, that it was hers. And rightfully so. She'd nailed that F sharp. And she'd held that note longer than any other girl in the Jazz Ensemble. Plus, Mr. C knew that she'd add a jazz lick in there for the show and top it off with a few well-timed dance moves. Amy had it goin' on and it felt good.

As the memory meandered, Amy saw the huge crowd that had shown up for the performance. Every seat in the auditorium had been filled, with folks standing along the walls and spilling out into the lobby. The crowd had cheered so loudly they'd shaken the building, and when they'd stomped out her name in roaring unison... Well, it just didn't get any better.

Somebody had told the local newspaper and a reporter had come out and done a write-up on all the kids. But it was Amy whose picture had made the paper, and the local television news had wanted to do a human interest story.

Local girl makes good.

Little had they known it would be the last time Amy was to be the heroine in any story. Because it had all gone south after that. Puberty had reared its ugly head. And hormones. And bipolar disorder — the family curse.

Everybody had thought that old family tree was filled with eccentric artists and musicians. Closer inspection revealed an entire tree of nuts. Lizzie had been struck at eight. In fact, Amy couldn't remember a time that Snotty Sis hadn't been weird. Amy had thought she was immune. Had known she was better than her sister. She'd dodged the bipolar bullet when eight, nine, ten, eleven had passed, and each year she'd been left unscathed. Then, *wham!* Slam you to the floor. Kick you in the gut. Wring you out and stomp you down. By the time her first period came, the roller coaster was making regular runs along the track — soaring into space and sunshine — then careening into black oblivion. Pay your ticket, grab a seat. Don't bother with the seatbelt…

As the blue light and jazz chords of her dream began to fade, Amy's mind started sinking into reality. *Oh God. Oh God. Had I? Did they? I'm such a slut. A trout. Oh God.* She was everything they said she was. A ho. A pros. And for what? The X was gone. Now she felt worse than ever. And beaten up. What had they done to her? Why was her crotch on fire and why did her body feel beaten with a bat? She wanted to die. Just die. And she had to go to school and face everyone. It was probably all over the Net by now. Her stomach lurched into a tight-fisted knot. She sucked in the room in an attempt to inflate her lungs. Vomit rose to the back of her throat. Oh, God. Everybody knew. They had to. Her body began to shiver involuntarily. What was she going to do?

"Amy, Mom says get up!" Lizzie popped her head into the bedroom with her usual crappy cheerfulness. Amy didn't know if she wanted to scream or puke.

"Tell Mom I'm sick. I'm staying in bed."

"Suit yourself," Lizzie yelled from the hallway. "But you know that won't fly."

Within two minutes, Mom was up and in the bedroom. "What's going on?"

"I really am sick. I think I'm coming down with the flu."

"If you don't go to school, you can't be in the recital tonight. Are you really too sick to dance? You've worked so hard for this."

The dance! Oh, crap. How can I miss the dance? It was all she'd been living for. But how could she go to school? No, no, she just couldn't walk the corridors at school and look at all those smirking faces judging her as she passed by. *Stupid. Stupid. Stupid.* Here was her chance to rehabilitate her reputation. Here was her chance to show another side of herself. The talented side of her. The capable side. Instead, Screw-Up Amy had showed up again. Even worse than that. Worthless Tramp, Piece of Shit Amy. And, without warning, Amy began to cry.

"Honey, what is it?" Mom's alarm was evident. Amy's moods might ping-pong all over the place, but crying was not in the typical repertoire.

Should she? Could she? Her mom's soft arm around her shoulders felt so warm and comforting. Maybe she could tell her everything. Maybe she could ask for help. Maybe she could— Could what? Tell what she did in the park? Explain that it wasn't her fault because she'd been high on Ecstasy? Describe how losing her virginity last night didn't really count because she'd been too high to remember much of it? Who was she kidding?

"I've just got such a headache..." Amy whispered.

"Well, honey, I'll bring you some aspirin and let you rest for a while. But you have to get up and get to class if you're going to dance tonight. And I'd hate to see you miss something you've worked so hard for, so let's get you up and going." Her mom walked into the bathroom and wet a washcloth. After wringing it out and folding it over, she laid it on Amy's head before walking downstairs for aspirin. Mom was nothing if not efficient.

As Amy lay feeling the iciness of the cold rag on her eyes and looking at the colors dancing inside her lids, her mind froze at the impossible decision that was just minutes from needing to be made.

Chapter Seven

If it hadn't been so mortifying, it would have been amusing, Amy thought. As she negotiated her way to class, Amy felt like she was in one of those horror movies where the fish-eye camera lens zeroes in on all the undead lurking in the shadows while the heroine walks the gauntlet seeking safety and salvation. Clearly, she mused, our heroine will not make it through unscathed, and surely, before the scene is over, somebody is going to die. For there she was, Miss Amy Miles, sorry-ass heroine of the whores, trying to maneuver past all those judgmental ghosts when all she wanted to do was make it into Cooper's class. But unlike that slash and burn movie scene, this was not breakneck special effects racing into the next change-of-tempo scene of relief. This was slow, ongoing, never-ending torture. This was every minute of the day lasting for eons as those digital numbers refused to let time move on and the leers of her classmates became etched permanently on their stony faces.

"Glad you could make it, Amy," chided Mr. Cooper.

Amy had no comeback today and could only slink into her chair. The entire class had become eerily quiet and that silence smashed into her ears like a wrecking ball into an abandoned building. 'Whore, whore, whore, whore...' Their judgment echoed into her veins with each beat of her heart. She knew what they were thinking. As she sat staring at the front of the room, Amy knew what their faces would reveal if they turned to look at her. And while they didn't turn, Amy knew every set of eyes was mentally checking out the latest class slut. She willed herself to breathe in and breathe out. To sit silently even though she wanted to scream and run. To act as if she had it all together even though she felt like her entire body would fly apart at any second.

For once, she appreciated Coop's droning lectures. His monotone worked like a salve on her battered nerves and time inched along. When the bell rang, Stacey jumped from her seat and sidled up to Amy as she left the room.

"You okay?"

"Yeah." Amy's voice cracked.

"Is it true?" Stacey looked straight ahead, walking beside Amy.

"Yeah." Amy, arms crossed over her notebook, squeezed her books closer to her chest.

"Why'd you do it?" Stacey searched Amy's face now.

"Don't know."

"Did they force you?" A deep furrow formed in Stacey's brow.

"Yes… No… I don't know. I don't remember much. I was rollin'." Amy looked away from Stacey and pulled her purse tighter onto her shoulder.

"Bummer," Stacey said in a low voice.

"That's an understatement."

"You could tell someone."

"Who?" Amy's voice dropped to a fierce whisper. "And what do I say, 'Oh, excuse me, I know I was rollin' with a bunch of freaks and they decided to rape me to pay for the Ecstasy, but I'm really not a whore even though I was too high to say no and really a victim here and you need to punish them but not get me or—oh yeah, my best friend Stacey—into trouble for taking an illegal drug in the park, and whatever you do, don't tell my folks'. How's that one sound to you, Stace? Don't I make a sympathetic victim? Don't you feel sorry for the way those assholes beat me up and handed me around? Don't you think the authorities will line up to help the stupid crazy girl? I don't think so."

As Amy's intense heat subsided, Stacey's shoulders

sagged, her face dropped and her voice seemed to fall an octave. "I'm sorry," Stacey murmured.

"Shut up."

"Hey, it's not my fault."

"It's not *not* your fault." And with that, Amy turned the corner and headed toward the bathroom. She just couldn't go to class right now and needed a minute to collect herself. Everyone in class was going to know and Ms. Grayson was so young that she often heard the rumors. The last thing Amy wanted was for Ms. Grayson to know what happened... After all Amy's hard work, after all her hopes for positive stardom. *I hate my life.*

Then suddenly, in the midst of her self-loathing, there stood J-J, talking to some girl from his class. Amy's heart flipped in her chest at the sight of him. Her breath caught in her throat. He was so long. He was so beautifully dark. He was so cool. It didn't matter that he'd passed her around. She deserved it, of course. But now he'd love her. He'd wanted her. He'd held her. Now she could be seen on the arm of the most gorgeous boy in school. It would be worth the shame of losing her virginity just to see everyone's faces when she laced her arm in J-J's. Then they'd see that she wasn't a slut. She wasn't a trout. She was J-J's girl and having sex with him was just what girlfriends do. There he was. Her salvation was within reach. It would be okay. It would finally be okay.

The crowd in the hallway froze as if in one of those stop-action commercials. Everyone pretended to continue their conversations, but no one moved as they stopped to stare at Amy and J-J and the best reality show on campus.

But Amy didn't really notice. For the first time since she'd awakened, Amy felt something akin to hope. She shifted her path from the bathroom to her boyfriend just as she shifted her focus from despair to relief. Relief to find J-J's arms. Relief to have her reputation restored. Relief to find escape from this nightmare.

When J-J looked up, his stunning, angelic smile twisted

into a smirk. His dark eyes traveled up and down Amy's body, stripping her, scorning her, savaging her. As they settled on to her shocked face, J-J's eyes flashed a quick, triumphant wink before he turned his back and walked away.

The kids in the hallway all began talking at once. Smirks, laughter and anonymous 'trout' remarks peppered the air as judge and jury declared Amy guilty and J-J 'too cool' for criticism.

Amy turned and fled campus.

* * * *

Blindly, Amy ran from school. Kaleidoscope colors danced within her eyeballs as if someone had just taken her picture with a flash. Her heart drummed in her ears so loudly she knew the sound would explode out her eardrums and blast into the world. Covered in sweat from running and panting, she nevertheless felt cold and couldn't stop shivering.

"I hate my life. I hate my life..." she mumbled between sobs. She felt as though an invisible hand had hit her in her chest, collapsing her heart and deflating her lungs... And she wished it had. She wanted nothing more—and nothing less—than to be dead.

Chapter Eight

The soft stroking sensation was the first thing that woke her up. As Amy's eyes fluttered open, it took a moment to realize that she was lying on the grass in the park. Danny lay beside her, quietly stroking her arm. Amy had been friends with Danny a couple of years before but they'd drifted apart as Amy had headed off in one direction and Danny in another.

"What's up?" Danny asked.

"Bad day." Amy's voice wavered.

"I'd say," he said, nodding to her books strewn in all directions as he pulled a leaf out of her hair. "Can I help?" Danny's gentle touch coursed up to her shoulder before slowly meandering back down to her hand.

"Doubt it."

"Would you like help?" The promise of…something — what? — lay beneath his words.

"What kind?" Clearly Amy didn't know much about Danny anymore.

"The mellow kind," he said as he produced a baggie of weed.

"Yeah, sure. That would be good…" she said, eager to escape her memories.

"But not here. I never smoke in public."

"So where?"

"My place."

Amy was still for a moment. She wasn't sure how much time had passed since she'd left school. Looking at the sun, it may have been quite a while. She needed to get it together and get back for the dance. But she felt foggy and drained.

A couple of hits might just make her feel better...or at least let her cope.

"Let's go," she said.

Danny's plan was to go to his place and take a few hits then head down the street to the arcade. He knew the guy at the ticket counter, they could get in for free and it was fun to trip with the lights and bells of the pinball machines.

Amy was up for the distraction. Her mind kept going back to the look on J-J's face when he saw her in the hallway. If only she were prettier. If only she were smarter, or sexier, or better in bed or...what? What would it take for him to love her? What would it take for him to look at her the way he had been looking at that other girl? What was so wrong with her that he couldn't love her?

Nobody was at Danny's place. They went to his room, took a few hits and talked for a while. But it was no good. Amy's pain was so overwhelming not even Danny's primo grass could take the edge off. When Danny offered his hot tub for a quick dip, Amy jumped at the chance to live dangerously and distract herself with the forbidden. Who cared anyway? It wasn't like she had anything else to lose.

* * * *

The entire act took less time than it had taken him to put the condom on. When it was done Amy sat in silence. Danny turned his back and fumbled to get the condom off. Neither spoke.

Amy flashed back to a time when she was nearly three. She had few memories from so early in her life, but this one was clear. She'd been playing around the stove as her mom was baking.

'Don't touch the stove, baby, it's hot'. Her mother had gently pushed her toward the kitchen door before turning back to the sink. In that moment, Amy had tried to grab a cookie off the cookie sheet her mom had just taken from the oven. Like it was yesterday, she could still feel the searing pain on her fingers as her hand missed its mark and grabbed the fiery cookie sheet.

As she sat in the hot tub her eyes glazed over with the same swirl of red stars that had replaced her vision that day in the kitchen. Again she heard her heart pound in her ears as she imagined her screams reverberating off the kitchen walls that day. '*Oh, baby, I said don't touch*', her mom had cried. Amy wished she could feel that same searing pain. She wished she could scream and scream until her head pounded and her eyes grew blind. Instead she was silent. Instead, she sat in a cocoon of shame and quiet humiliation. '*Oh, baby, I said don't touch*'. But she had.

Danny got out of the hot tub and went inside. Amy put her clothes back on over her wet body. In a few minutes Danny came out and handed Amy a colorful pill.

"Here," he said. "A present. I've been saving it for a rainy day, but I think you need it more than I do."

"Thanks." Amy popped the pill into her mouth. In just a few minutes she knew she could escape this awful day.

"You okay?"

"Yeah." Amy smiled for the first time that day.

"I didn't mean…" Danny's head was down, his voice low.

"It was no big deal." Amy shrugged, surprised that her shoulders responded to her mental commands as if what she was saying was really true.

"I didn't want to take advantage…" Danny just couldn't let it go.

"Shut up."

"But…"

"Don't you get it? I'm just the local trout—" The edge in her voice surprised even Amy.

"Amy, don't talk like that. I think you're cool…"

Oh God, he *liked* her. He really liked her. What a fool. What a total idiot. Did he not get what a screw-up she was?

"Just shut up. Okay, Danny? You didn't force me. You're not in trouble. Let's just go to the stupid arcade."

As they walked, Amy saw herself lying in the road, hit

by a bus. Yeah, that would be good. That might just be dramatic enough. She saw herself laid out in her blue dress. No, no, her black pencil skirt and boots. Yeah, she looked good in that. There she'd be, in the street, her blonde hair shining on the pavement. And J-J would come out when he heard all the noise and see her there, dead. Then he'd be sorry. Then he'd wish he'd loved her. In fact, he'd run up to her. He'd lift her poor, lifeless head and cradle it in his arms. He'd cry—oh yeah, he'd actually cry when he saw her beautiful, innocent face in such soft repose as she lay there dead. And he'd be sorry. No, no. She wouldn't be dead, just gravely injured. And as he held her, *thinking* she was dead, she'd softly moan and J-J would realize what a mistake he'd made by letting her get away. He'd know that he really loved her, couldn't live without her, and he'd take her in his arms, follow her to the hospital—walking right past skank-girl without a glance—and there she'd revive and they'd live happily ever after—

"I said, you okay?" Danny's voice cut into her daydream.

The hits had done Amy no good but the X was starting to kick in. Amy could feel that pull into the pit diminishing as the tingle of Ecstasy began to flow through her veins. As they stepped into the arcade the bells, beeps and whistles interlaced with the neon lights and flashing bulbs to lift her off the ground and float her around the room. *Oh yes, oh yes. Escape is at hand. Paradise is near...*

But, but...what's this? Suddenly things began to change. Vibrations from the bells and beeps started to roll toward Amy in a tsunami of pounding sounds. The flashing lights morphed into electric monsters rearing up with lightning intensity and bolted right at Amy's nose. Claws of crackling light zapped Amy's eyes and slapped at her raised hands like fiery hot pokers. She tried to pull back, tried to scream, but the beating sounds and exploding lights were everywhere, pounding on her senses and ripping away the walls of the arcade. In a second Amy flew out of the arcade and into a netherworld of floating colors and jolting sounds. Each different wave of sound took on an otherworldly nature, tearing at her skin, grabbing her hair and prying off her face. Amy screamed and fought but the sounds were everywhere, enveloping her in death and destruction, ripping apart every limb, every fiber of her being so that she knew, if they succeeded, she would be no more. Amy grabbed for some handhold to save her, but the colors swirled and flowed in her way, blocking her escape and forcing her into the depths of this tortured, agonizing world. Amy opened her mouth to scream again, but no sound came out and the colors drained into her mouth, filling her lungs and smothering her in their rainbow oppression.

And Amy collapsed.

Chapter Nine

An antiseptic smell jolted her senses. A hard bed jammed against her hip. Sharp light jarred her closed eyelids.

"She's awake!"

The teen voice making the announcement wasn't anybody Amy knew. As she struggled to make her mind focus, an older woman in blue scrubs leaned over the bed.

"How are you feeling, Amy?" This other, deeper voice was also not familiar.

"Tired…"

"I'm sure. You'll probably sleep the rest of the night. Do you want to get up and go to the bathroom?"

Amy shook her head and tried to open her eyes.

"Okay, just push this button if you do and I'll help you. You can't get up alone."

Amy closed her eyes and fell back into a blissful state of nothingness.

* * * *

"Time to get up." The voice pounded in Amy's ears. "Sleep time is over."

The fog in Amy's brain continued even as she heard the footsteps of her human alarm clock leave the room. She rolled over and pulled the blanket over her shoulder.

"She's not kidding, dumb shit," said the girl in the bed next to Amy's as she threw back her blankets and began making her bed. "If you want to eat, you'd better get your ass out of bed."

Tall and heavy-set, the girl slipped into backless slippers

and began padding into the bathroom. "I'm not kidding. Up and at 'em. I'm being your friend here."

What bed was this? Who was that girl? And why wasn't she home? Suddenly Amy's eyes flew open, but she stayed within the safety of her blanket. She had no recollection of coming here or...or anything really. She searched the room, looking for clues. The thick fog in her brain made the sorting of these puzzle pieces laborious. The room looked like a cross between a hospital and a dorm. Three beds lined the wall at intervals. At the end of each bed were three shelves and two drawers. The other two girls had their own blankets — obviously their own — but aside from that there was nothing personal in the room. Where was she?

Almost silently, the girl in the far bed crept toward the bathroom then, seeing that it was already occupied, turned back around. Amy felt her more than saw her, heard the water already running in the bathroom and felt the girl creep back to her bed. Still in the throes of confusion, Amy imagined the girl was a cat slinking across her bedroom.

"Okay, Miss Amy. Are we finished with our beauty sleep?" The voice began talking before the body even entered the room. That body was short and thin, with long brown hair sprouting strands of gray. Her skin was slightly wrinkled at her eyes and drooped with the softness of age. She looked friendly and talked in that singsong way some new mothers do.

"What's going on?" Amy asked as the woman walked up to her bed.

"Well, Missy, you did a number on yourself the other day. I'm Marina," she said, touching the name tag pinned to her flowered scrubs. "Glad to find you back with the living — you've been sacked out for two days."

"Two days? What? But the dance..." Amy's brain tried to make sense of it all. "I've got to get to school."

"Don't think so. There'll be no school for you for a while. You are in the company of the Serene Meadows Psychiatric Facility and you're going nowhere for some time, dear.

Now let's get you up and get something to eat. We're strict about breakfast around here, so you'd better wash up and get a move on."

Her sentence was punctuated by the longest explosion of personal gas Amy had ever heard escaping from behind the bathroom door. Cat-slink girl hovered on her bed, dropping her head and making retching motions into her sheet. Amy herself felt an acid taste rise up her throat and threaten to burst forth.

"Stop it now," warned Marina as she walked over to cat-girl. "You're fine. Just take a breath."

Just then the tall, heavy-set girl came out of the bathroom as if nothing had happened. As if she hadn't just opened the door and released a sewer smell that could drop a mountain of maggots. As if she hadn't just grossed out everyone within a ten-mile radius. She'd brushed her dark, straight hair and pulled it into a sloppy bun with a scrunchie, but was still in her pajamas. Her short sleeves revealed massive white gauze bandages on each forearm. Whatever had happened to that girl's arms had been wicked, thought Amy. The girl caught Amy's stare and offered a shy smile as she emerged from the bathroom.

"Ah, Amy, this is Francesca. Francesca — Amy." Marina made introductions like she was at some social event, not sitting in the middle of a psychiatric hospital. "And on the bed is Katrina. She doesn't like to talk. Okay, Amy, your turn for the bathroom. Hurry up and I'll be right back to escort you to the cafeteria. Just so you know, you may not leave your room without someone to accompany you."

You've got to be kidding, thought Amy as she imagined walking into the gas chamber that Francesca had just created. But Marina's frown sent a warning shot in Amy's direction and she decided to obey until she knew more.

Amy staggered into the bathroom, her feet more wobbly than she'd expected. She took one look at the toilet and turned away. There was no way she was going to risk any unwelcome noises escaping her body while an audience was waiting outside. Sometimes she'd held it all day at school—nothing would stop her from doing that today. Besides, she was calling her mom. She'd be out of here soon.

Her eyes moved to the counter and a plastic tub with her name on it. Inside was a toothbrush, small tube of toothpaste, a small plastic brush, trial-sized deodorant, a feminine pad, a hotel-sized bar of soap, washcloth and towel. Like they'd expected her. Like they figured she was staying. This had to be a dream. There must be some mistake. She needed to call her mom and find out what the hell was happening. She'd ask for a phone when she saw Marina again.

As soon as Amy stepped out of the bathroom, Marina was waiting. "Come on, Amy. Just follow me." Marina placed her hand at Amy's back to guide her but didn't actually touch her. Her two roommates fell in behind them and they headed out of the door.

The whole place smelled like the convalescent hospital her grandmother had stayed in before she'd died. It looked like it too, as they passed one open door after another. Amy quietly checked out the rooms. They were laid out just like her room, with three girls in each. The rooms at the far end held teens while the rooms closer to the lunch room had younger and younger girls so that the last room held seven- and eight-year-olds.

Two long tables were surrounded by plastic chairs in the drab blue, softly lit lunchroom. At the end of the tables an open window was well lit, if not welcoming. Lined up under the florescent lights were Styrofoam bowls of Cheerios and oatmeal. Packets of sugar were set off to the side and tiny containers of milk rested in a bowl of ice. Orange juice filled half of the miniature Styrofoam cups lined along the far side of the window next to the green gelatin and soda crackers that rounded out the selection. Some choice, thought Amy, walking past the food.

"I'd grab some if I were you," chirped Marina in her happy little singsong. "Meds are next and they can be tough on an empty stomach."

"I'll pass," said Amy.

"You were warned," Marina said, but not unkindly.

Amy sat in silence in the room as the girls around her ate. Francesca hovered over her bowl like a vulture over a rotting corpse, her bandaged arm draped around her food. Every few seconds she'd look up and Amy got the distinct impression that she was waiting for Amy to grab her food. Odd bird, Amy thought and smiled to herself.

"You should eat," Francesca said between bites.

"I don't do breakfast."

"You'll get sick. I'm being your friend here," she garbled as she shoveled in another spoonful.

"Sicker than this?"

"You know what I mean." Milk dripped down her chin as she talked without ever stopping the regular, rhythmic beat of her spoon hitting her teeth.

"Actually, I don't. I'm just trying to figure it all out. How long you been here?"

"Two weeks."

"And your arms are still that bandaged? Jeez, girl, you must have done a number on yourself."

Francesca pulled her arms down under the table.

"Oh God, I'm sorry, I'm sorry. That was none of my business. I'm just freakin' out here. I thought I was supposed to be starring in a dance recital tonight—last night—two days ago— Oh God, do you get how confusing this is? How scary this is? How do I get the hell out of here?"

"You're kidding, right?" A smile curled the side of Francesca's mouth and her eyebrow shot up.

"No. I'm not. Why would I be kidding? How do I go home? I don't belong here."

"None of us do." Francesca sat up straight and Amy detected just a hint of sarcasm.

"No, really—" Amy began to protest.

"Really." Francesca's answer carried a strong period at the end.

The girls sat in silence for several minutes as Francesca

resumed her vulture impression over her cereal. She got up, got another bowl and sat down across from Amy. As she watched Francesca settle back into eating, Amy's cloudy confusion began to burn off like so much overcast sky. In its place rose the burning light of awareness and fear. This was no dream. This was no joke. She was trapped in a freakin' psych ward and didn't even know how she'd gotten here. Amy could taste the fear as it filled her nostrils and the back of her throat with the acrid stench of bile. She had to get out. She had to get home. But how?

"So, here's the deal." Francesca seemed to have read her terror and had moved closer to Amy. "You're here on a seventy-two-hour hold. They really don't want to keep you any longer than that unless you have good insurance. Otherwise they want to send you home to Mommy and Daddy just as badly as you want to go. Play nice. Follow the rules. Take your meds and you'll be home smokin' pot and being a bitch to your folks again by tomorrow night — tops."

"Really?"

"Unless you screw up, yeah."

"And if I screw up?" Amy didn't want to even ask the question, but that bile taste had found permanent residence in her throat.

"You'll go on a contract and can stay here for up to a month. If you can't get it together after that, they move you to a residential facility. Unless, of course, you really screw up and melt down first — then it's 'Go straight to jail, don't pass Go, don't collect two hundred dollars.' So, don't screw up." Francesca's eyes kept watch over the room as her voice quietly gave up the keys to escape.

"And how exactly do I avoid that? Screwing up, that is?" Amy tried to keep the panic rising in her chest from spilling out through her throat, but even she could hear the fear.

"Not easily. Trust me, they may smile and sing to you, but they're all Nazis here. Just do what they say when they say it — no matter what."

59

"That should be easy."

"Yeah, right," snorted Francesca as she began her watchful hover again.

"Amy!" The voice over the loudspeaker startled Amy mid-conversation. Francesca pointed to a second window Amy had failed to notice when she'd walked in. A large, heavy-set woman with 'Melba Lou' on her name tag gestured for Amy to come to the window. Two girls were already lined up in front of where she was to stand.

Amy watched with horror as each girl stepped up to the window and was given a small paper cup filled with an assortment of pills. In turn, each girl took the pills, swallowed them with the water provided, then opened their mouths and stuck out their tongues, waving them up, down and side to side as the woman peered around inside with a flashlight. It had been bad enough when her mom had forced her to take her meds, but this was...was... The violation was so egregious, so invasive, that Amy was shocked when no one said or did anything. She looked over at Francesca for some reaction but the girl just raised her eyebrow slightly and shrugged. Clearly complaining was not in Amy's best interests.

As she picked up her pills, Amy tried to take the first two out to swallow. She always swallowed them two at a time, sorted by size and color. She reached in to comply as quickly as possible when—*whack*! Melba Lou slammed her water bottle on the counter with such force that Amy literally jumped off the floor in fright.

"What do you think you're doing?" Melba Lou's girth was exceeded only by the size of her voice. Amy clenched her legs together, terrified she was going to pee on the floor.

"I was taking—"

"I do *not* have time for you prissy girls to play with your meds. I've got work to do—*today*—not tomorrow. Now *swallow* them and open up."

Amy took the entire pill cup and poured it into her mouth as she'd seen the other girls do. But as she gulped a large swig of water, her gag reflex took over and, involuntarily, she spat the whole thing down the front of her scrubs and onto the tray of meds awaiting the other girls in line. Violently, uncontrollably, Amy choked on the water that went down her windpipe.

"Are you kidding me?" Melba Lou's rage rose as she stood up behind the counter, rearing up in her fury, and before Amy even knew it, her full bladder was convulsing and pee was running down her leg like a leaky water hose. Despite her unrelenting coughing, Amy began lifting her feet like a Clydesdale stallion as she ran up an invisible air-path away from the puddle of pee. As her foot rose, her slippers sent drops of urine shooting through the air, splashing on all the girls standing behind her in line. They began to scream and dart away from Amy's urine spray gun.

"I'm sorry. I'm sorry. I'm sorry! I'm sorry!" Amy's voice rose to a shriek between her hacking coughs as she began to grab and pull at her hair. Her heart beat so hard she thought the vein in her neck would explode. She gasped for air between hacking coughs and hysterical apologies while panic overtook her and her vision turned black. "It's not my fault! It's a mistake. I didn't mean it! Let me go home!" Amy's cries wound up louder and louder and faster and faster until she couldn't stand it another second and let out a long, wild, ear-jolting scream. In her blackness, she felt herself being tackled to the ground. Then there was nothing.

Chapter Ten

"So do you want to talk to me?" Amy's mom stroked her arm as Amy lay restrained in the bed. "I just don't know what to do here anymore."

"Take me home, Mom." Amy's voice was so soft and quiet Mom had to lean in close to hear her words. When she did, Amy saw the pain on her mother's face and thought, for sure, that her mom would understand and take her home. It really hadn't been her fault. She couldn't use the bathroom. She couldn't swallow all those pills. Melba Lou was mean. No, really. Melba Lou was a bitch. And Amy hated when people talked mean to her. She was a nurse, for Pete's sake. She was *supposed* to be nice to patients. What kind of attitude was that? She couldn't help it that she'd peed. She'd been scared. She'd choked. Who wouldn't have? And besides, if her mother hadn't put her here in the first place none of this would have happened. That was it. It really was her mother's fault. *Mothers are supposed to protect and take care of their children. They're not supposed to call the cops on you. They're not supposed to abandon you to the loony bin. They're supposed to love you. No matter what. That's their job.* And her mom was doing a piss-poor job of it since Amy was stuck here, in this bed, in freakin' restraints.

As she watched the wave of emotions dance across her mother's face, Amy let her own fear and pain show on hers. Her mom needed to see how sincerely she wanted to go home. Mom needed to see that Amy knew she'd made mistakes. But so had Mom. They needed to forgive each other and move on. Amy saw her mother's eyes melt with the love that she remembered since her first memories and she knew that her mom understood how wrong this whole situation was. She'd have reached out to hug her mom for the pure joy of their mutual understanding if only she could get her hands loose.

"Oh, baby," her mother whispered into Amy's ear. "You have no idea how much I want to take you home."

Amy looked up at her mom and saw tears streaming down her mother's face. Mom got it. Her mother realized what a mistake she'd made to put Amy in the hospital. She got it and she'd take her home now. Amy knew she had to get it together. But so did Mom. She needed to trust Amy and quit bossing her around. Amy would do better. Clearly Mom had made her point and Amy understood. As she watched her mom's tears, Amy knew that she and her mom understood each other, understood their own responsibility in this mess and that they each would get it together when Amy got out.

"But I can't possibly take you home. You're just not safe." Just then a sob escaped from her mother's throat, but not before Amy's wail rose to cover it in a wave of rage. *What the hell did you just say? You're not going to take me home?*

"Don't leave me! You can't leave me! Don't do it! I'll kill myself if you leave me here! Mom! Mom! Mommy — please, I beg of you. I'll do anything. Mommy! You can't. You can't leave me..." Amy thrashed and fought the restraints as a pure, primal animal wail rose from some deep, unknown place in her soul.

But even as she screamed her mom got up, turned her back and began to leave.

"I beg of you, Mama. Don't do this! Oh God. Don't leave me." Amy frantically thrashed in the bed as she willed her cries to lasso her mother and drag her back. As if in response, her mother stopped mid-step. But then she straightened her shoulders, lifted her head just an inch, and walked out of the room.

* * * *

It seemed like an eternity before her mother walked back into the room. Amy had screamed, then cried, then whimpered until she had no more strength left to protest. Along the way she had seen her mother's sweater draped over the back of the chair by the bed and realized that she hadn't actually left. There was still a chance. There was still hope.

Then Mom stepped back into the room.

"I've asked them to remove your restraints while we talk," her mom began. "I assured them that you will behave and stay in the room. Will you?"

Amy nodded. She was exhausted and numb. She couldn't have done anything if she'd wanted to.

Her mother sat next to her in silence while the attendant walked in and snapped the releases open on the restraints. Amy pulled her arms then feet out of the soft cloth braces and rubbed her wrists and ankles as her mother pulled the chair close and began speaking in low tones.

"Amy, I don't think any mother has ever loved a daughter as much as I love you." It was the beginning of her mom's regular how-much-I-love-you speech and, at first, Amy allowed her usual glaze to begin to shield her eyes. But suddenly she stopped and looked at her mom. Really looked. Like a slow-mo camera, her eyes panned across her mother's face in a zoom lens close-up. When had she begun to look so tired and old? When had she gotten all those wrinkles? And what was that heaviness that seemed all around her? *But really, why is she sad when I'm the one on trial here?*

At that moment, her mother's sigh grabbed Amy's attention again. "But I doubt many moms have worried about their child as much as I worry for you. You are in real danger. You are going to kill yourself and I can't stop you. I'm a good mom. I'm a dedicated mom. But I'm just a mom."

What the hell was that all about? Modesty was not her mother's strong suit. What was she talking about?

"I know a lot of 'mom things' but I don't know a lot of medical things or psychological things that I think somebody has to know to save your life. Dad agrees. He's smart. He knows a lot of things, but he doesn't know what to do for you any more than I do."

Amy began to sense where the conversation was going and needed to sidetrack it before something awful happened.

"Wait, Mom. Wait. I get it now. I'll change. I'll be good."

"Oh, sweetheart. If only it were that easy."

"But it is." Amy reached for her mom's hand. She needed to touch her mom. She needed to push the truth of her promise into her mom's skin so that Mom could feel, really feel, how sincere Amy was in her conviction.

"No, it's not. This is not about your willpower. This is not about a character flaw. This is not you being a screw-up. This is about a terrible, terrifying condition that is taking over your life and destroying you. This is about a monster that is doing battle for your soul... And right now, it is winning."

Amy's mom was still talking, but Amy's mind was racing ahead. How could she stop this conversation? In an effort to convince her mom to trust her, Amy replayed her memories of one scene, then another, from her myriad actions of the last few weeks—but it was hopeless—there was nothing that warranted trust. She was doomed. Amy let go of her mother's hand.

Her mom's voice rose to her consciousness again as Mom continued her endless thoughts. Normally Amy would be impatient with her mom's monologues, but at this moment she relished the time so she could think. So, maybe, she could find a detour from this horrific path they were descending.

"It is going to take an army of professionals to give you the weapons you need to beat this monster," her mom droned on. "You are going to need to make an arduous journey to obtain the power to live beside this danger. And I simply don't have the tools to help you. I could be selfish and keep you with me. The truth is, that's what I want to do…"

Then do it! Amy's thoughts screamed back at her mom. *Then do it. Why can't you do it if you want to? You're the mom. You're the one calling all the shots here!*

"But you will die," her mom continued, as if she'd heard what Amy was thinking. "And I could never live with that."

"But, Mom…" Amy reached for her mom's hand again like she was reaching for a life preserver.

"No buts. Listen to me. They have a residential facility they want to send you to."

"What's that?"

"It's a place where you would go to live with other girls. They have psychiatrists and therapists there twenty-four-seven. You'd go to school, and get therapy and get meds… and get help. It also has fun things like rock climbing, horseback riding, camping, canoeing…" Her mom's voice trailed off. Then she took a breath and seemed to turn a corner in her thoughts. "I won't tell you it's like camp, because it's not."

Amy tried to focus her eyes and concentrate on what her mom was saying. She knew, in her heart, that this was a done deal. She knew she had to pay attention, but she couldn't get her mind to settle into her body instead of leaping into a stratosphere filled with anguish and terror.

Rock climbing and therapy? Was she freakin' kidding? And yet… And yet…

"But I will tell you that some parts of it might be fun." Her mom's voice slipped into an irritating white noise as Amy's thoughts ping-ponged around in her head.

"And I know some parts will help. Amy, I think this is our last chance. I think if we don't do this, you will do something bad to yourself. I'm afraid if we don't do this I'll be burying you within the year."

Amy couldn't respond. Her parched mouth could not form one word of response. Air had ceased to flow into her lungs. She saw the love and pain on her mother's face. She heard the tears caught in her mother's throat. And yet…

And yet… And yet there her mother stood. Stood and said she was sending Amy away. Giving her up. Goodbye, crazy girl. So long, drama queen. Amy closed her eyes and felt the air begin to flow down her windpipe and into her lungs.

As she breathed, the air began to circle within her chest cavity. Rock climbing? Horseback riding? She'd always wanted to learn to horseback ride. Year-long camp? Off on her own? Away from all the nagging? No, really — away from the nagging? That might not be so bad.

No sooner had those happy visions danced across her eyelids than other, darker visions began to intrude. The arcade. J-J in the hallway. J-J in the park. The bouts of uncontrollable rage. Her dreaded pills rolling around in her hand. Danny's scared look when the colors began to attack her. The broken shower door. The grocery bag she tied around her neck. Her total lack of control. Her cyclone-like life. Rage. Fear. Panic. Loss. *What do I really have here? What do I really have to lose?* It was a fresh start. It was a chance. Maybe her last chance.

Suddenly, everything was clear.

"But, Mom, don't you get it?" Amy reached over and gently touched her mother's hand. "Residential is where I belong. Do you have any idea how crazy it is inside my head?"

Chapter Eleven

An ambulance transported Amy to the residential facility. *Green Acres Academy* was etched into a large granite stone beside the entry drive. They had to be kidding. Amy had watched late-night TV and seen that lame old-school sitcom about the city girl in the country. The show sucked, but now the tune started playing in her head. Was this 'her' place? This was so stupid.

The attendants bumped and banged the gurney as they got it out of the ambulance. Amy was getting pissed. She could walk, but they insisted that she stay in the gurney. Now she realized it was because they had tied restraints across the bed. They'd said it was to keep her from bouncing while they drove — but it was clearly to keep her a prisoner until they could deliver her to the 'school' — also known as the 'nut house'.

From her perch on the gurney, Amy watched the watercolor salmons and peaches of the sunset disappear as the attendants pushed her away from freedom and into... what? Amy had no idea what lay ahead of her. Aside from happy pictures of smiling campers, she had no clue what Green Acres was really about. She wasn't even sure how she'd gotten to this place in her life, but here she was, being pushed through double glass doors into a residential psychiatric facility. Funny, how glass doors marked the threshold between freedom and confinement. Somebody had a sick sense of humor.

On the other side of that threshold the rich wood paneling in the foyer and large oak doors behind the receptionist gave the place a stately, tranquil appeal. When the ambulance drivers had gotten their signatures and dropped off Amy's satchel, she was helped up off the gurney and over to a polished oak bench where a young blonde woman in a Green Acres polo shirt—Kelly green, of course—was waiting for her.

The hospital had made a list of things and her mom had gone home to pack. When she'd returned with the bag, the hospital staff had told Amy to kiss her mom goodbye, and had told them both that they wouldn't be allowed to see each other or talk on the phone for at least a month…and only then if Amy earned the privilege. It had seemed like a lame threat back there, but now, as an iron vise of fear began to bear down on Amy's solar plexus, it felt terrifying to think she would be cut off from her family for that long.

At some secret signal the woman next to Amy stood up. "Come on, Amy, let's go."

She walked Amy through the beautiful oak doors behind the receptionist. It was only when those doors slammed shut with an echo-y clang and automatically locked behind her that the chill of realization gripped Amy's spine and made her jump. Oak veneers hid the fact that those doors were solid steel inside with locks that snapped shut via a remote button at the warden's desk. And despite the thick taupe carpeting and rich wood veneers everywhere, the clank of that lock bounced off the walls and echoed around the room like a sonic boom. This was prison. *Prison.* Dress it up all you like, the sound of that lock was final.

Tears leaped up to the backs of Amy's eyes, but she gritted her teeth and breathed out slowly in response. She was not about to cry because a stupid door slammed. Never.

The blonde woman guided Amy into a small room to the left of the doors. Another, taller, older woman with gray hair that looked like curly steel wool was already seated on a stool in the room.

"Stand up, feet apart. Face me," said the older woman in a quick, no-nonsense manner. "Lift your arms out straight and stay that way until I tell you to move."

Amy had to concentrate as hard as she could to make her arms obey.

The younger woman patted Amy down, running her hands through Amy's hair before moving to shoulders, arms, chest, waist, hips, thighs, legs and feet. As first one place then another on her body was touched, Amy closed her eyes. She needed to block her vision, not speak and stay still. Too much information was pounding into her brain.

"Take off your shoes," the older woman instructed in that same quiet, authoritative tone. Amy complied.

"Your jacket."

"Your shirt."

"Your pants."

"Unhook your bra."

Amy tried to follow the instructions, but her hands shook too violently to manage the hooks. She tried again, but again failed.

"May I?" The younger woman's eyes offered a softness as her hands hovered close to Amy, awaiting permission.

Amy could not speak, but offered the slightest nod before the young woman unhooked her bra then gently held Amy's wrists and brought Amy's hands up to her chest. "Here," she instructed. "Cover your breasts like this while I take your bra."

"Now turn your back to me and hold your hands out straight." Amy didn't know if she could remain standing much longer – dark flashes were beginning to dance before her eyes and the women's voices seemed to be backing down a long tunnel.

"Amy? Are you listening?" The voice that broke through was not unkind but seemed to be coming from very far away. "With your back still to me, drop your panties to your ankles and squat down," commanded the older woman. "Amy? Amy?"

The younger woman stepped up again. She remained behind Amy but touched her shoulder. "Drop your panties, honey," she guided. Then, as Amy complied, she gently but firmly pushed Amy down to the floor.

Amy's mind circled back to the hundreds of pliés she'd done in dance. Her muscle memory responded with a graceful grand plié until the older woman's voice jerked her from her dream. "Cough three times."

"What?" Amy's daze was so deep that the words were no more comprehensible than if they'd been in Swahili.

"Stay in that position and cough three times."

There, squatted, her hands covering her breasts, her panties down around her ankles, Amy searched her brain for what the woman wanted from her, what was being asked of her. She desperately wanted to comply with whatever request these people were making, but the meaning was garbled and bouncing around her brain with no place to land.

"Amy, look at me. You need to cough. Like this..." The younger woman was still behind Amy with one hand on her shoulder, but her gentle touch guiding Amy's chin up to her and sharp coughing sound helped Amy connect the dots and provide the physical response that was being requested.

"Pull your panties up and put these on. You can step behind that curtain." The younger woman handed Amy a pair of blue scrubs and pointed to a rough green curtain hanging from a rod in the corner of the room. Once dressed, she handed Amy a cup. "There's the bathroom. Go pee for me and bring it back out here. Oh, and leave the bathroom door ajar, please."

Amy had to hold the doorjamb to steady herself as she walked into the bathroom. The older woman had left, but the young woman was waiting outside the door when Amy emerged.

"Let me walk you to your room, Amy. You'll start at Orientation—we call it 'Calming'. You'll be there several weeks, depending on how fast you learn the rules and cooperate. You have some nice girls in your room with you who know the rules, so you'll be fine. Once they inspect the

clothes your folks sent, you'll wear your own clothing—
that should only take a day or two. As you earn privileges,
you'll be able to have some personal items. I know this all
feels invasive, but it's for your own safety and the safety of
the other girls. Lights out is at nine. Have you eaten dinner
yet?"

There was a pause in which Amy knew she was supposed
to say something, but she wasn't sure what. She looked into
the woman's eyes to see if a clue to the answer lay there.

"Amy, have you eaten yet?"

Oh, that's what she wanted. "Yes. Yes," Amy replied softly.

"Then let's just get you settled." The woman stopped
outside the dormitory room. "Amy, tonight will be the
hardest. It just is. Get through tonight and it will be easier.
Really. Do you need to use the bathroom? No? You won't
be able to use it in the middle of the night. Still no? Okay.
Oh, by the way, my name is Pearl. Ms. Pearl. Now, come
meet your roommates."

Chapter Twelve

Amy willed her feet to move one past the other as Ms. Pearl escorted her into the room.

Two sets of bunk beds lined the bare white walls. Three of the beds were disheveled and each was draped with a silent, staring teenaged girl. Several plush toys, pillows and individual blankets defined each bed and its owner as unique in the sterile room. Off the confines of the beds, the room was empty — no pictures on the wall, no curtains lining the mini-blinds, no rugs on the floor. Along the other side, a bank of drawers and shelves delineated the individual girls' 'closets', each containing two drawers at the bottom and two small shelves over the top. Sweaters, pants and toiletries were neatly arranged on the shelves in full view of anyone walking into the room. Three sets of shelves housed a couple of pictures of family in homemade frames of craft foam or cardboard. One set of shelves was completely bare — apparently awaiting Amy's arrival.

"Yo, girl," said a girl with wild hair, freckles and soft brown skin from the top bunk. "I'm Mallory. Welcome to hell."

"Mallory, that will be an A ticket for you," replied Pearl in a quiet tone.

Mallory immediately got up off her bunk. With her long, leggy walk and quiet confidence, she crossed the room to accept what was clearly a punishment and wrote 'A' beside her name on the dry-erase board by the door. As she passed Ms. Pearl on her way back, she smiled and shrugged while giving her wild mane a little toss then hopped back up on her bed.

"Amy, this is Mia." Ms. Pearl's hand gestured to a tiny, fragile, doll-like Hispanic girl huddled on the bottom bunk under Mallory. Mia barely raised her eyes as she said, "Hello," and Amy couldn't help wondering what had beaten this girl down so severely that she couldn't even speak.

"And this is Emily." Emily shot up from the bottom bunk then stopped at Ms. Pearl's warning glance. She stood as if tethered to her bed, with her hand thrust forward for a handshake. Amy wasn't sure what she was supposed to do. *Shake hands? You've got to be kidding.* But there Emily stood, with her bright red, braided hair and porcelain skin, looking like a kid waiting for the parade to round the corner. Amy expected Emily to start jumping up and down at any second. Even in her anxious stupor Amy couldn't leave the girl hanging, so she reached out and brushed her outstretched hand. As she did, another worker stepped into the room with folded bedding and a pillow.

"Oh, thanks," Ms. Pearl said as she took the bedding. "Here are your linens. It's late. Make the bed. We'll show you the proper way to make it tomorrow." Ms. Pearl turned and addressed the group. "Ladies, I'll give you another five minutes to get to know each other and talk a little. Don't take advantage of the privilege. Lights out in five."

As soon as Ms. Pearl had walked out, Mallory walked over to Amy. "So what brings you to lovely Green Acres?" Mallory gave Amy a soft elbow in the ribs while she picked up the sheets and began to make Amy's bed. "Don't think this will become a habit. You just look sort of out of it and I want to get to bed. So like I said, what you in for?"

"Too much X."

"My mom kicked me to the floor for drinkin'. Didn't mention to the cops that she's a lush. Doesn't matter. Didn't want to stay with her anyway." Mallory's voice was monotone as she quickly fitted the bottom sheet of the bed before reaching for the folded top sheet. "Now Emily here is our little Aspie. Her folks got all the money in the world but don't like the idea of a little autism at their social events, so they plunked down a big wad of cash and locked their little baby in Green Acres. Yippeee."

As her story was being told, Emily closed her eyes, flashed a silly grin and bobbed her head up and down like a bobblehead doll. She didn't even notice when Amy rolled her eyes at her before returning her gaze to Mallory.

"Over there is Mia." Mallory pointed to the beautiful, fragile Hispanic girl spreading her tiny frame as far as it would stretch across her bed. Mia's eyes, however, were still red and her nose was blotchy from an apparently recent cry. "She's our resident cry-baby. She's the oldest of twelve kids and I guess she just misses the wail of babies in the house, so she just has to do it herself." Amy caught Mallory's smiling wink tossed Mia's way, but Mia dropped her head onto her bed anyway.

"So'd you kill anybody?" Mallory finished tucking the blanket into Amy's bed before opening the covers in a mock invitation.

"No!" Amy stepped back away from this outrageous accusation.

"Good." Mallory smiled as she jumped up on her own bunk in one smooth motion. "That means I don't have to worry about you killing me in the night. Good night. Oh, you're the last one out of bed — turn off the light."

* * * *

As soon as the lights went out, all the girls became quiet. Amy laid herself down and had begun to pull the blankets up when the first wave hit her. The sheets felt strange — cold, a little scratchy. She pulled them up to her nose and breathed in at one place, then another. They smelled wrong. Not like home. She loved to rub the silky on her blanket to go to sleep, but this blanket was a rough cotton with no edging or lining on it. Her fingers stopped rubbing and curled up to touch her inside palm. Her feet searched the bottom of the bed to find a familiar spot, a cozy feel. But it was hopeless. There was no reassuring smell, no comfortable touch, not one familiar sense to grab on to. And the second wave hit. *I'm alone. Thrown away like so much trash. And not just for today or tomorrow. For a long time. Maybe forever. Not talk to anyone for a month? I could die in this month and no one would even know.*

Her chest began to tighten in on itself as it recoiled from the touch of the covers. *I miss Stacey. And Kairyn. And, I'll admit it, J-J. I want to go to my own school with my own friends and fall asleep in my own bed.* Her legs pulled up into her chest on their own as they sought to find comfort in a tight ball of familiarity. *I want my dad...and even stupid Lizzy. I want my mom. Please God, let Mom feel how wrong this is and come and get me and take me home where I belong. Let Dad come get me. That's it. Please, God, get me home. I just want to go home. Please, God. I beg of you. Please, God. Please...*

It wasn't until the first tear trickled into her ear that Amy even realized she was crying. But then it was as if that tear turned on a torrent that would not stop. Amy rolled onto her stomach and buried her face in her pillow to try to dampen the small sounds escaping her building anguish, but despite her best efforts to squelch the outpouring, her sobs rocked the bunk bed, and the more she tried to stay quiet and frozen, the more they heaved their way past her convulsing chest and out of her throat, until she had no strength or feelings left and fell into a tortured sleep.

Chapter Thirteen

The blast of the buzzer slammed Amy's heart onto the ceiling before her eyes even opened. Immediately the other girls started piling out of bed, then turned and began to make up the beds behind them. Everyone was silent.

"Make your bed," Mallory mouthed to Amy as she pointed to Amy's rumpled sheets and blankets. Her heart still ricocheting from the morning alarm, Amy hung over the side of the bunk and tried to adjust the covers as best she could.

Like choreographed dancers, the girls finished their task and stood at attention beside their beds. Instantly a staff member poked her head into the room. "Okay," she said before ducking back out of the door. The girls fell into a relaxed stance as Emily scooted off to the bathroom.

"You can talk now," Mallory informed Amy. "You're fourth in the bathroom 'cause you're the newest. Just pee. Later you can go back and get ready, but first run is just to pee so nobody explodes while they wait."

Mallory rummaged through her drawer for clothes, but stopped and refolded every shirt she discarded. "They're really strict about order, so keep your bed and drawers neat if you ever want to get any privileges. Messiness is the fastest way to get a ticket."

"Ticket?" asked Amy

"Yeah, some sadist thought it would be fun to name the punishments after old-school Disneyland tickets. In the old days the crap rides were A-ticket rides. Bs were better and then Cs — well, you get the idea, until the E rides were the best. You know, like Space Mountain or Tower of Terror, although they didn't have those rides back then, I don't think. Anyway, here A tickets are for nothing offenses — you can buy them off with points or pay the time in a heartbeat. But an E ticket will get you in trouble with the cops or thrown in Isolation. Don't worry, they'll explain it all to you in the handbook."

"What handbook are you — "

"Amy," Mallory interrupted quietly but urgently, "we can talk, but you gotta get ready. It's your turn for the bathroom. You don't have clothes today, but brush your teeth and hair before she gets back."

By the time Amy got out of the bathroom, the staff member she'd seen earlier was at the door. "Move it, Amy," she said, but without any real admonishment. "You have chores to do."

The girls fell into line behind her and walked back to the main lobby where Amy had been last night. Instantly Mallory grabbed the vacuum and started to attack the carpeting. Mia and Emily each took a dust rag and, walking to opposite sides of the room, began moving lamps and books as they dusted the furniture. Amy wasn't sure what to do.

"Stay with me," the staff member said as she handed Amy a dust rag and pointed to a low coffee table. "For the rest of the week you and I are a team. I'll help you get oriented to how we work around here and answer any questions you have about procedure. My name is Ms. Brooke. You will address me as 'Ms. Brooke' and respond to my directions with 'Yes, ma'am' or 'No, ma'am'. Do you understand?"

Amy nodded as she tried to dust the table that Ms. Brooke had indicated.

"I didn't hear you."

Amy looked up at the woman, startled by the sudden tone in her voice.

"I didn't hear your answer, Amy. How do you respond?"

"Oh, yes, ma'am."

"Good. In the future, if you forget to answer like that, you will get an A ticket for the infraction. Do you understand?"

"Yes, ma'am." Amy's voice was low but her heart was beginning to race as she slowly pushed the dust cloth across the table. What was she getting into? Yes, ma'am? Were they kidding?

"We'll teach you how to make your bed later today. You will immediately arise at the buzzer each morning, make your bed and be ready for inspection within five minutes. Only after inspection may you talk or use the toilet. You'll then have ten minutes to dress before beginning a.m. chores. After chores you'll have breakfast and meds. Now, please repeat to me the morning routine."

Amy froze. She'd had no idea there was going to be a test! She had been floating in and out of attention and now had no idea what to say. Her eyes searched the room for help from the girls, but no one looked past their chores.

"Amy?"

"I'm sorry, I sorta missed that."

"Sorta missed that who?"

"Ma'am. I sorta missed that, ma'am." Amy's palms were beginning to perspire and little spots of black were dancing in front of her eyes. *Concentrate*, she told herself, *concentrate. Don't get labeled as a screw-up.* But her breath began to come fast and flooded her ears with a roaring that kept her from hearing the instruction Ms. Brooke was rattling off.

"…minutes to dress before a.m. chores. Then breakfast and meds…"

Listen, girl, listen!

"So, tell me…"

"Get up, make my bed, be quiet. Get dressed, don't be anywhere alone, do chores…"

Ms. Brooke's nodding reassured Amy that she was stumbling through the checklist with some success, so when she faltered, Ms. Brookes' corrections were gentle and supportive.

"After breakfast I'll give you the Orientation Workbook. Your job is to memorize all the rules this week. There will be a test. We are strict here so that you know exactly what's expected of you. Eat when you're fed, take your meds when they're given, sleep when you're told, do your work, study in school, get along with your peers, obey the staff. You'll also have group therapy every afternoon and will meet with your therapist for individual therapy three times this week and then weekly for as long as you're here. Abuse, substance abuse, anger management and sexual abuse therapy groups meet at different times each week. You're expected to choose an appropriate group and attend. I know it feels like a lot of rules, but you'll catch on. Life here is pretty simple — follow the rules and you earn privileges, disobey and you earn consequences. Plain and simple. Choose your path. Choose your life. It's up to you. As soon as you pass the test, you'll leave Calming and move to the next level. You can begin earning privileges then and life will feel better, Amy."

Life feel better? I doubt it. What was I thinking when I told Mom yes? This is a horrible place and I've made a terrible mistake. How the hell do I get out of here?

"Excuse me, ma'am." Amy braved the question as she needed to grab the only lifeline she could think of. "Will I be able to write home?"

"Yes, you may write this afternoon."

Chapter Fourteen

At some silent signal, the girls put their cleaning supplies away and fell in line behind Ms. Brooke, who led them to the cafeteria. Inside, the girls washed their hands at a basin by the door then lined up beside the trays.

"Take whatever you like," instructed Ms. Brooke to Amy alone. "But eat whatever you take. No food leaves this room. You will be searched. Sit with your room. You may talk, but once you're seated, you may not get up without permission. Raise your hand if you need anything."

Amy's stomach flip-flopped as soon as she laid eyes on the food. She did *not* want to eat, but memories of her last experience at institutional breakfast made her think twice. She put a bowl of Cream of Wheat on her plate along with five packs of sugar and a carton of milk. Orange juice rounded out the tray. Then she waited for Mallory to sit down and followed after to be sure that she sat in the correct place.

Like a tightly coiled spring, Amy sat and ate her breakfast. Even using her spoon felt like a new, foreign skill. She was afraid to do anything wrong. Spill her juice, slurp her milk. The rules hovered like giant birds of prey, circling, watching, waiting to swoop down and grab Amy the second she let her guard down and offered an opening for attack. She didn't know how the cereal was ever going to find a place to stay in the tight knot that had become her stomach.

"Take a breath." Mallory used her cranberry juice glass as a pointer to get Amy's attention. "You're here to stay for a while, so take a breath and relax."

"It's not so bad. We could be friends." Emily's disgustingly cheerful offer reminded Amy of her sister, Liz. Amy had to smile at the crash of conflicting emotions that fell over her at Emily's request—revulsion at the offer and the mirrored image of Liz, followed in rapid succession by a heartache for home and, who'd have thought, the actual missing of her sister! *No wonder I'm in the loony-bin, I'm actually missing Lizzie!*

"No! I won't! You can't make me!" *Crash! Splot!*

Everybody ducked as a cereal bowl flew across the room and smashed against the wall. Three staff members went running after a heavy-set dark-haired girl who had jumped up from the table and was screaming at the top of her lungs. Arms flying through the air, she was batting away something around her head as she heaved whatever plates and trays she could grab.

Ms. Brooke got to her first, grabbed the screamer's arms across her chest and, thrusting her foot between the girl's legs, forced the girl down on the ground in one swift motion. Two other staff members immediately joined the fray and in a quick, coordinated move they adjusted so that one person took each arm while a third sprawled across her legs.

"They're coming! They're coming! You can't make me! They'll fry you, I say! They'll fry you!"

"Food to dorm!" yelled one of the staff from her position on the floor. Instantly, all the girls got up with their trays and silently walked out of the cafeteria and toward their rooms. Amy's legs crumpled under her as she tried to stand up next to Mallory and it was only Mallory's quick support under her arm that kept Amy from collapsing.

In total silence, the girls marched to their rooms, trays in hand. Just before the roommates entered the threshold of their door, a big, African-American girl barreled past Mia, knocking her into the wall and nearly upsetting her tray. Mallory and Emily stepped up beside Mia, but other than that, no one seemed to do anything. The offender kept walking while she ran her hand through the back of her short, spiked hair and slowly lifted her middle finger in salute, never slowing her pace.

After she passed, the other girls rounded the corner and slipped into their room. Once there, they sat on the floor and continued to eat.

"Just ignore Kelly," Mallory began. "She's bad news. Stay as far away as you can."

Amy looked over at Mia, whose eyes were welling with tears, but as she reached her hand out, she caught Emily shaking her head, a sad smile on her face indicating that Amy should stop.

"That was Molecule Myra in the cafeteria," Mallory said with a smile. "She's psycho and her meds aren't working—"

"Or she's not taking them..." said Mia, head down, voice a small whisper.

"Probably not," continued Mallory. "They dampen her appetite and you know how much Myra likes her food."

Mia's knowing look seemed to indicate that she'd recovered and was back with the group.

"Anyway," Emily broke in, smiling like a Cheshire cat, "it makes her cuckoo and she goes off whenever the voices get too loud. She thinks Molecule Men are after her. It's always Molecule Men trying to fry her. She starts yelling back or running away from them..."

"You'll get used to it," Mallory said reassuringly as she took a bite out of her toast.

"Besides," Emily said with a grin, "we get to eat in our rooms, and that's fun."

"Yeah, but don't spill." Mia's voice was louder than Amy had ever heard it as she pointed to Emily's coffee cake crumbs next to the tray. "I've got vacuum duty and I won't get a B ticket because you're a slob."

In the meantime, Amy hadn't taken a bite of her food. Her hands were still shaking too hard to lift her food, and besides, her throat had locked down and frozen.

Chapter Fifteen

Dear Mom,

Let me come home. I beg of you. I don't belong here. It is way, way worse than I thought it would be. If you saw it for a second, you would get me right away and not let me be in a place like this. I know I was bad. I know that I was disrespectful. I get it. You've made your point. Just let me come home and I'll be the best daughter a mom could ever have. I know I've said it before, but I mean it this time. I don't belong in this place. I'm terrified out of my mind. I'll do anything, Mom, anything. Please come save me. I swear I'll die if I have to stay. Save me. Please.

Love, Amy

Amy reread her letter before folding it up and putting it in the envelope she'd been given. Because she hadn't earned the privilege of a pencil, the letter was written in red crayon. As much as she'd tried, Amy hadn't been able to make her letters neat or really even legible with a crayon on blank stationery. But Mom had to know. She just had to get word to her so that someone — anyone — would come save her from this nightmare.

Amy licked the edge of the flap and handed the sealed envelope back to the staff. There, in front of Amy, the letter was addressed and a stamp affixed to it.

Amy let out a sigh as she walked away. There. The SOS was sent. Help would be coming.

* * * *

Dear Diary,

I can't believe I have to write in crayon. How humiliating. But they gave me my diary back and promised it was private, so I need to write.

I've never been so terrified in my life. This place is a cross between a zoo and the worst horror movie you've ever seen. Girls fight here every day. Not your usual call-each-other-names fights. No. Your I'm-going-to-knock-you-to-the-ground-and-rip-your-throat-out fights. Somebody calls an "E ticket offense" over the intercom and staff come running. They throw the offender down on the ground, restrain her and take her away — usually for days. I'm so afraid I can't stop shaking. I'll do anything, ANYTHING to avoid having that done to me. Oh God, it's so scary here.

But what scares me the most is what they DON'T see. Kelly is tormenting Mia, but the staff and teachers never notice. Andrea is bullying Sonja but no one says a word. Some of these girls are gang members, and if their tattoos are telling the truth, they've killed somebody. And they won't let me call. I know it's because they don't want parents to know how bad it really is in here because if anybody's parents saw inside here for even a minute, they'd never let their kids stay. I'm so afraid I'm going to die. I'm so scared.

Amy

Chapter Sixteen

Over the next couple of weeks Amy learned the gazillion rules that governed Green Acres and formed the basis of the G-A Way. Whatever the hell that was. She was horrified to learn that every aspect of her waking and breathing was regulated. Peeing before check-in was an A ticket offense. Farting in a manner that stank up the room was a B ticket — a 'gross or lewd act' they said. Good grief! How did they expect her to control her farts? All her clothes had to be folded neatly and put in drawers or on the shelves. Anything misplaced would be confiscated and mailed home. She was even only allowed five pairs of granny panties — no thongs, no bikinis — apparently some smart-ass had used them to try to hang herself so now Amy had to look like some old fart under her clothes.

Each morning Amy rose at six, made her bed, did her chores, ate the same Cream of Wheat for breakfast and went to class. English, algebra, humanities, earth science and PE — although PE was a joke. Amy wasn't on a high enough level to be allowed outside, so she had to just walk circles around the gym for PE. *Like a mouse in a maze*, Amy thought as she circled the room. *What other experiments will they subject me to?*

After academics came therapy. Chemical dependency classes, PTSD desensitization, anger management, rape recovery, abandonment issues, abuse recovery, dealing with depression, eating management. *Pick your flavor of the month, we got cures for whatever ails you.*

Homework and afternoon chores followed. Amy soon learned that the reason Green Acres didn't need a custodial staff was that they forced the girls to do everything—absolutely everything—to keep the campus clean. Already she'd scrubbed down all the cupboards in the kitchen and orange-oiled all the lobby floors. She'd even written to her mom telling how she was being used as slave labor, but she had still heard nothing from Mom.

Dinner was followed by a processing group where the girls got to spill their guts ad nauseam and Amy thought she'd puke. Group was followed by showers and hooray! hooray! twenty minutes of free time—the only free time of the day—before lights out.

No question about it—this was prison.

And there would be no escape until she 'Climbed the Cs'. As Amy studied the pages in the book, she nearly threw the damned thing. *Couldn't you just barf? Is there anything more ridiculous than cutesy naming the only escape route out of this hellhole?* Orientation was renamed 'Calming'. 'A moment to settle the mind, cool the body and begin to focus on the task at hand', read the workbook. *Who writes this crap?*

The next step was to 'Commit'—'to realize what was holding you back and commit to fixing it'. *Who wanted to know? Who wanted to look? What were these people smoking?*

Knowing she wasn't allowed to deface the workbook, Amy drew a line of square boxes in the corner—allowed scribbles reserved for students diagnosed with attention deficit disorder. Amy wasn't diagnosed but she drew over and over and over the lines anyway as she pushed her frustration out onto the workbook so she wouldn't just throw the book across the room at this craziness. Some idiot wanted her to memorize this crap and *she* was the one locked up?

Then, oh and this was rich—'Conquer'. In the next step, inmates—oh, right, 'students' learned to begin to weed out bad behaviors and extinguish old patterns so that they could move to the 'Control' step of the program. *What? 'Control my behavior', you say? Duh! Why didn't I think of that?*

'Create' did make Amy stop for a moment. She had to

take a breath when she read about the possibility of creating a new life, a purpose-driven life where she took charge of her behavior, she took charge of the outcomes and she chose the direction of her success versus letting her disease choose for her. Could that really be a possibility?

Just then Kelly walked over to the teacher's desk and grabbed a new pencil. They were only allowed to write with the little, short pencils that were poked into church pews or in cups at the miniature golf course, and only teachers could sharpen pencils – to half-points – so everyone had to get up during class to exchange pencils. This was Kelly's third stint at Green Acres. She was a violent sociopath plus oppositional-defiant, and therapy simply didn't stick. Her mom was dead, her father an alcoholic who had abandoned her after repeatedly raping her and beating her up, and Kelly was permanently pissed. Half black, half Irish and as mean as they come, she'd been a big shot at home – pun intended. Amy was sure that she'd probably shot someone – or at least seen her boyfriend shoot someone– in LA, where he was a gang member and she was his bitch. The irony was that Kelly was a lesbian and had it bad for Mia.

As she walked past Mia's desk, she dropped a pea-sized paper onto the seat between Mia's legs, and the look on Mia's face indicated that she knew what the note said and didn't want to read it. Amy looked for a second into Mia's eyes and could have sworn she saw tears forming. To Mia's right, Andrea pushed her long, dark hair back from her face so she could smirk at Mia. Bulimic, with a bad oppositional-defiant streak, Andrea was Kelly's shadow, relishing her leader's conquests and more than willing to take the fall should actual consequences come Kelly's way. Mia's shoulders flinched at Andrea's smirk, but she never turned her gaze in the other girl's direction. Just then Kelly turned back from the pencil box and Amy's eyes flew back down to her workbook.

'Conclude' was the last step in the process – and the ticket home. 'Conclude business at Green Acres, maintain commitment to conquering old habits and creating a new life and leave with a calm that was not possessed on arrival.' Amy started counting the steps on her fingers—Calm, Commit, Conquer, Control, Create, Conclude. Six freakin' steps? Were they kidding? When was she ever getting out of here? How could she possibly keep living in this prison? Amy's heart sank into her stomach as she counted the time it would take to escape. They said the average stay was a year. Amy had thought that was a joke. Two weeks—a month, tops, had been her prediction. And yet, looking at what it took to 'Climb the Cs', it appeared that the game was rigged and escape holes closed. It felt hopeless.

In fact, if it weren't for Mallory, Amy would have wanted to kill herself. But Mallory could make her forget she was at Green Acres.

* * * *

"Check out Molecule Myra," Mallory whispered on another day as she and Amy made endless laps of the gym. "Looks like her friends have come to visit again."

When Amy looked over, there was Myra, arms aflutter, walking and engaged in the most animated conversation with the air next to her. Amy smiled over at Mallory as they continued their conspiratorial stroll.

"Did you hear that they fired Doug?" Mallory got in close to deliver this bit of news.

"Who's Doug?"

"You know, the guy who drives girls to the airport."

"Oh, him. Why?"

"He made a pass at Gloria."

"What? Are you sure? I bet Gloria made a pass at him."

"That'd be my guess. But I heard she said he said she was cute and to look him up when she got out."

"Eww—gross."

"I know! Think about it. Just really think about it! Isn't it the grossest thing you could ever think of?" Mallory ran her fingers up and down the front of her body like a cross between a horror picture and a cover girl before making wild, shuddering movements that made Amy laugh out loud.

Just then the girls passed Jordan, who had found her way over to the badminton nets and was trying to cut her wrist with the clip from one of the nets.

"No, no, no, Jordy," cooed Mallory. "Don't do that. Run. You'll feel better."

Jordan looked up blankly and kept rubbing the clip across her already badly scarred arm.

"What gives?" asked Amy.

"Jordy's one of the reasons we have to use baby pencils. She peeled off the metal band at the eraser end to make a knife. She's a cutter and she's got it bad. Needs to 'vent' every day, she says, and gets wild if she can't. You should see her when she's not focused on cutting—she's articulate and really cool, but then she gets like this. They keep mixing med cocktails for her, but look at her."

"How long she been here?"

"Two years."

"Two years?"

"Don't panic. She's the senior member of the group. She'll be here until she ages out."

"So really? They fired him?" Amy needed to change the subject, as Jordy's long stay had set off a panic and she couldn't continue that conversation.

"Huh? Oh yeah! Walked his ass right off the property. They really don't fart around with anybody coming on to us—you know how they have to protect our virginal honor here at Green Acres." Mallory had taken on a hilariously prim tone as she held her legs together to the knees and tried to walk with her right hand holding an imaginary tea cup—pinky delicately raised.

Amy got the giggles, which turned into a full-blown laugh-fest as she and Mallory let the stresses and frustrations of the day explode in peals of laughter that echoed throughout the gym. Yeah, life was better with Mallory around.

* * * *

Dear Diary,

Mallory taught me how to play solitaire today.

We were allowed a half hour of games because our unit did a good job this week. She told me that it would be good to learn to do something I could do alone. Mallory knows how I hate to be alone and how afraid I am here. Well, maybe not as much as before. But I really don't know how I could have thought coming here was a good idea. I was so stupid.

Anyway, I'm pretty good at cards and am getting better.

Sonja and Sam are lovers. They sneak into each other's beds all the time and you can hear them going at it. It's so gross. I don't know why staff doesn't hear – I wonder what they do when they're not checking our beds. Probably playing cards themselves.

Anyway, sometimes when it's loud, Mallory will start doing sex pantomimes in her bed. She is hysterical with all her facial expressions and throwing her arms dramatically into the air... She can even get Mia laughing from the bottom bunk and Mia can't even see her!

I can't believe how tired I am. Nobody cares if you tell them, they just tell you to buck up. But with school, and issues classes and chores...and everything...there isn't a minute to sit and rest. I'm surprised girls don't drop over dead. Don't they die from overwork on chain gangs or something? I betcha somebody does soon. That'll show them. Anyway, I'm tired and gotta sleep.

Amy

Chapter Seventeen

"So, I heard that you talked back to Ms. Avery today. Do you want to tell me about it?"

Sometimes Amy wished she had a dollar for every hour she spent in therapy. She was sure that kind of wealth would solve all of her problems—then she wouldn't need therapy in the first place!

Unfortunately, that wasn't the real world. This was. And now, behind closed doors with Ms. Prudy Casey, MFT, she had to explain why she'd talked back to Bitch Avery.

"She ripped my bed apart after I just made it!" Amy was doing everything in her power to keep her voice calm as was required by the G-A Way, but the injustice of the whole thing was about to overwhelm her emotions.

"And why do you think she did that?

"Because she's a bitch."

"'Want to try again?"

"Because she's a *real* bitch."

"Three's a charm." No matter how she tried, Amy could not rattle Prudy, although why anyone would call this thin, sleek, athletic beauty 'prude' was beyond Amy. But there she was, sitting with one leg tucked up under her in her rolling chair, holding her pen like a cigarette, gently smiling at Amy's refusal to answer the question.

They sat in silence for a few minutes before that smile forced Amy to smile back against her will.

"Okay, okay, so maybe she's not a *real* bitch. Maybe I didn't make it right. But I tried."

"Did you?"

"Yes!"

"Yes?"

"Well, no. But I was tired. Do you have any idea how hard they work us here? It's not fair. I think child labor laws are being broken. I bet if I called Child Protective Services they'd have a fit about what you're doing here!"

"Are we getting a little off topic, Amy?"

"What do you mean?"

"Did you try your best to make the bed or not?"

"But, Prudy, I just can't do my best every morning. I was tired. And I had to pee. And besides, it's stupid. I'm just going to get into it again tonight."

"What about pride in your actions?"

"What about it?"

"Amy, seriously, this incident illustrates two issues that have already arisen here. First, that you'd rather run than try, and second, that you won't take responsibility for your own actions."

"That's not true!"

"What part of it isn't true?"

"All of it."

"So you're saying you have no responsibility in Ms. Avery tearing apart your bed despite the fact that one, you knew the rules, two, had been taught how to make your bed properly and three, knew the consequences of not complying?"

"She could have cut me a break."

"You could have done what was expected of you."

"I just can't do this all the time!" This time Amy could not control the emotions screaming up through her throat. "It's just so hard. There's no break. There's never any break. It's just work, work, work. Process. Process. Engage. Attend. Focus. Step up. When the hell's step down, relax, chill, kick back?"

"You're here to change your life. That's not really something you can take a break from. Changing old habits—unproductive habits—takes diligence, hard work and dedication..." Prudy let her voice trail off as they sat quietly for a moment.

"Let me ask you this," she continued. "Do you really *want* to change your life?"

"Of course I do."

"Wait, Amy. Don't give me the automatic this-is-what-I'm-supposed-to-say answer. Stop and think a moment. *Do you want to change your life?*"

The intensity of Prudy's gaze made Amy stop for a minute and consider.

"Some of it, maybe," she began. "But some of it that everybody else wants me to change is fine with me."

"Like what?"

"Like not making my bed."

"Because…"

"Because it really doesn't matter. It really doesn't."

"Okay, and what else?"

"Smoking pot. I *like* pot. I like the way it makes me feel. It's the only thing that helps me relax."

"I get that, Amy. But is it worth it knowing that, statistically, for bipolar and other mentally ill people, smoking pot pretty much assures you won't make it in life? That mix of pot and meds is just a lethal combination for success."

"Exactly, Prudy. I also shouldn't have to take my meds. No one would make me take them if they knew how they made me feel. I know there's something in the Constitution about cruel and unusual punishment — meds are definitely cruel and unusual punishment. You never get to feel good. You never get to feel high or happy or ecstatic. True, you don't feel suicidal or out of control or manic. But I'm not sure the price is worth it."

"I understand," Prudy said. Then, looking at Amy's disbelief and disgust, she continued. "No, Amy, I really do understand how you feel. We know that the meds we give you have wicked side effects. They make you feel like a zombie. Some give you Parkinson-like shakes. They cause weight gain. Others can give you diabetes. It sucks. No doubt about it."

"Yeah..." whispered Amy into her folded knees.

"But without meds and therapy, one in five people with bipolar will kill themselves, did you know that? Or that people with untreated mental illness die about twenty-five years earlier than others, make up twenty-six percent of the homeless and represent seventy percent of youth in the juvenile justice system? Those are pretty awful statistics."

"Yeah, well I'll take my chances."

"Do you really want to take those odds?"

"Yes."

"Yes?"

"*Yes*! Don't you get it? This is my life! Not yours. Not Mom's. Not anyone else's, and I want to do what I want to do."

"Okay, but then there are consequences for that — the least of which is your bed being torn apart."

"Crap."

"Yes, *crap*. Amy, you were dealt a rotten hand. You have a very difficult disorder to fight and you will have to fight it every day of your life for the rest of your life — no breaks, no vacations, no kick backs. But, despite that, you *do* have control of your behavior. And no matter how much it sucks, there are consequences for our actions. Do the crime — pay the time."

Prudy sat silently for a moment as if waiting for Amy to speak, but, defiantly, Amy kept her mouth tightly clamped. They sat in silence for a full minute before Prudy continued.

"If you're willing to pay the price, then I suppose that is a choice you can make. But I believe you're made of stronger stuff. I believe that you can dig deeper, find your inner strength and make the most of the hand you've been dealt. You simply need to quit living in denial, take responsibility for your life and get on with it."

As if to accentuate her point, Prudy tossed her pen onto her desk then turned to put her face close to Amy's.

"Pull up your big girl panties and just do it."

Amy opened her mouth to protest. Then stopped and sank back down into her knees. Prudy sat looking at her until she saw Amy's body relax into itself. "I think our session is over now."

Amy walked to the door, then turned back to look at Prudy. Amy lifted her finger and opened her mouth to speak, then stopped, dropped her hand and walked out before quietly closing the door.

* * * *

Dear Diary,

It's so lame here, I can't stand it! You're not allowed computers, but HAVE to play this dumb video game. They want me to move through this kingdom by controlling my breath and blood pressure. Can you believe it! Control my blood pressure? And they have me locked up.

Anyway, the whole thing pisses me off. You have to slow your breathing to keep this dumb balloon in the air. If you breathe too fast, it flies up in the air and is lost. If you breathe too slow, it crashes into the rocks and pops. It's a trap. I started to do it and got excited because it was working and then, BAM! It floated too high, so I accidentally held my breath and popped the damned thing. Who thought up this stupid game anyway?

I seriously don't see the point.

Amy

Chapter Eighteen

As Ms. Avery tightened the strap of the harness, Amy rubbed her sweaty palms onto her sweatpants. *Get it?* she said to herself. *Sweatpants. Sweat on pants. Oh shit.* For it didn't matter how she tried to distract herself with corny jokes and stupid distractions, she was going to die. Right here. Right now. And nobody was going to give her a break or save her from her fate. She didn't really care that they'd explained all the safety precautions. She didn't care that they said it had a better safety rating than bowling. Bowling, for God's sake. She didn't care that she had a harness on. Dead was dead.

"Helmets on!" Ms. Avery barked out orders like a staff sergeant and obviously relished the opportunity to really — no, *really* — boss the girls around. Amy's hands trembled like fall leaves in the wind as soon as she tried to secure her helmet.

"Here, let me help." Mallory's voice was absolutely sympathetic as she grasped the clasp of Amy's helmet and swiftly clicked it into place.

"Mallory! B ticket!" shouted Ms. Avery over the excited voices of the girls. "That's Amy's job."

"But she needed —" Mallory began.

"Another B ticket for talking back!"

"Shit."

"That's three — want to try for detention?"

"No, ma'am."

"Better." A tiny smile flickered across Ms. Avery's mouth, although it never extended up to her steely eyes.

Amy saw the smile and, without looking at Mallory, she

slightly moved her right hand a half an inch in her friend's direction. There, her index finger and thumb slowly came together in a circle while her other three fingers straightened up together in the sign-language symbol for 'b', which the girls used as their private signal for 'bitch'. Without the hint of a smile, Mallory casually brushed her nose as if to scratch an itch—the return signal for 'right'. Without missing a beat, the girls readjusted their equipment and stepped up into line.

Amy's heart was pounding in her ears. Before her loomed a rock wall twenty-four feet high. Rough-faced, multicolored edges and crevices blocked any easy access path of handholds that Amy could trace. Yellow- and salmon-colored spotlights lit and shaded the structure in a way that, Amy supposed, was meant to look natural and dramatic but only appeared that much more sinister to her terrified eyes.

It was Step-Up time and this was the test. Were the girls willing to commit to Commit? They had finished their orientation—Calming—and were moving up to the second step. Each girl had completed her workbook, memorized the rules, begun to show evidence of maintaining her temper and emotions, learned to treat her peers and professionals with polite deference and made progress toward committing to mental and physical health. Now each had to show a commitment to move past her comfort zone and risk-take for her own good and the good of the group. And climbing this freakin' wall was the G-A Way of proving that commitment.

Squinting, Amy concentrated on Emily's path as the girl effortlessly scaled the wall like an ant on a doorjamb. *Easy for her to do. Emily doesn't have the sense she was born with.* Mia, on the other hand, was hovering three feet above the ground, loudly weeping as she lay plastered against the side of the wall. With one hand stretched far above her head and locked onto a rock, she was frozen in fear. *Oh God,* begged Amy, *please don't let me humiliate myself that way.*

Since the first day she'd arrived at Green Acres, Amy had lived her life in a straightjacket—tightly wrapped, confined and desperate to escape the straight-jacket hold of the rules and regulations that were part of the G-A Way. She did everything in her power to never make a mistake. After the episode with her bed, it was getting more and more difficult. Avery was on her butt, always looking for a chink in her armor. Amy remained vigilant, following orders the first time she was asked, keeping up her grades, doing her chores. Every night she fell into bed, totally exhausted from the unrelenting tension of the day. Every night she awakened with nightmares of forgotten rules, or hostile girls or sadistic staff, and lay in silent terror until she could calm down and go back to sleep, but she wouldn't give up. She intended to play this game and win. She was determined she'd move through the steps faster than anyone ever had and get the hell home. And she was pretty much on her way. Now she needed to—

Mia's piercing scream stopped everyone in their tracks. Kelly had started climbing next to the sobbing girl and now was feigning an apologetic look as she ever so slowly removed her heel from Mia's fingertips. With pain overriding her fear, Mia pulled her hand off the rock and out from under Kelly's foot and jumped off the climbing wall.

"I'm so sorry, Ms. Avery," began Kelly. "I never saw her hand there. I just needed to catch my balance and stepped on the rock. It was the only foothold around."

Kelly's words told one story, but her smirk said something entirely different. Amy's breath caught in her throat. She saw the menacing glance Kelly threw Mia's way and the terrified cower with which Mia responded. Standing beside Mia, Andrea stood watching, barely suppressing a smile as her gaze shot from Kelly to Mia and back again—couldn't Ms. Avery see what was going on?

"That's a C ticket for you, Kelly," Ms. Avery commanded. "You may not have intentionally hurt Mia, but you clearly were not keeping track of your mind and body, which was the point of the exercise. Take a seat for fifteen minutes then we'll see if you get a second chance to complete the step."

"Oh, but, Ms. Avery!" Andrea raised her hand as if she were in class and turned to Ms. Avery, looking every bit like a church choir angel. "I saw what happened, and clearly Kelly had no choice — she just slipped, that's all."

"Good try, Andrea," countered Ms. Avery. "But Kelly knows her body and she simply didn't belong in Mia's personal space. Period. Now, Kelly, get to the bench."

Kelly winked at Mia as she stepped over to the bench. Avery never even paid any attention to the exchange and, clearly, hadn't intimidated Kelly in the least.

"Amy, you're up!" Immediately Amy stepped forward and Ms. Avery attached the hook onto her harness.

"Go, go, go, go!" Just as they'd done for every other girl to face the wall, her teammates shouted encouragement to Amy as she placed first one foot then the other onto the rock holds and began her ascent.

The rock surface felt warm from all the hands that had just followed the path in the last half hour and the rough sandiness of the handholds had a surprising feeling of comfort. Amy's shoulder muscles and wrists strained hot while she pulled her weight up to the next level and she heard the scratch of her shoe as it rubbed against the rock in search of a foothold. Her breathing was starting to come hard now and she could feel her heart beating in her ears. She reached for the next handhold, her ear pressed against the side of the wall under her small bike helmet, amplifying her heartbeat while the wall soothed her hot face with its cool stoniness. Terrified that she'd mimic Mia's outburst, she'd had her eyes closed as she began her ascent. But now she could feel that she was ascending rapidly and she needed to see where to find the next handhold. She had to open her eyes to find the safe place. The lights and shadows of the room bounced off the backs of her eyes and filled her brain with warm color. She breathed in the clean mineral smell of the rock and tried hard to reach up for the next cool space higher up.

As she did, Amy lifted her right leg to find a foothold. Just then, her foot hit a wet spot and she slipped, lost her brace and began to fall. The weight of her body pulled her right hand away from the wall and her left leg scraped down the wall as the fall sandpapered off the skin inside her thigh. But she couldn't even cry out as she fought for a foothold on the right before she lost it entirely and fell from the wall. She looked down to find a safe place to land her foot and began to swoon as she grasped the enormous distance between herself and the safety of the floor below. She sucked in a sharp, knife-like breath as she flailed frantically. Her foot kicked and pushed again until it suddenly landed with a satisfying 'thud' onto another hold while, at the same time, her right hand found a small fingerhold right above her head. Her fingers pressed into the rock until their tips turned white and the pain from the pressure shot hot arrows up the insides of her wrists. Amy pressed her body against the wall and panted for air.

"Good save, Amy! Now keep going. You're not done yet!"

Even from this distance, Amy could hear the condescension in Ms. Avery's voice. That was easy to say from her safe vantage point with both feet on the ground. Whereas plastered against the wall, shaking and panting, Amy didn't even know how to make any one of her limbs move. Her shaking began to grow in intensity, like the rumble of an earthquake as the tumbling waves get closer and closer. Her eyes clamped shut, her lungs beginning to scream for air in rapid, gulping cries. She couldn't take a step up or down. Without warning a great sob escaped from her throat.

"Get it together, Amy. Don't wimp out." Avery's command was loud and sharp.

But it was too late. Within seconds it became clear that Amy was going nowhere and Ms. Avery pulled the rope, released the pulley and lowered her down...to defeat...to humiliation…to failure.

Dear Diary,
It just doesn't matter how hard I try. I screw everything up.
Stupid Emily can get to the top of the wall like she's a freakin'
monkey climbing a tree. But me? Never! Oh, Mallory was all
sympathetic and nice, but BFD! I don't want her to feel sorry
for me. And – more pity – they gave me the step up to 'Commit'
because I 'put forth my best effort.' But once, just once, I would
like things to go my way. Why don't I ever get a break? I'm
trying here. I'm trying. But I just can't do it. I'm only at freakin'
'Commit!' I want to go home. I'll do anything to go home. I want
to go home.
Amy

102

Chapter Nineteen

"Amy! Phone for you!"

One of the privileges of moving up to Commit was a phone call each week, and this was Amy's first. As she hurried to the hallway where the phone bank was, Amy had to smile at her excitement. Not too long ago she'd lived on her cell phone and this would have been one of dozens of calls she'd have gotten today. Now this was her first call in a month.

"Hello, Amy..." came the familiar voice on the other side.

"Mom?" The tears instantly filled her throat and fogged her voice, but Amy didn't care. "I miss you, Mom."

"Hi, honey, it's me, too," Dad chimed in.

"Dad? Mom? I miss you."

"We miss you too, honey. How are things there?" asked Dad.

"Better. I've made a friend..."

"Oh, I'm so glad. What's her name?" Mom questioned.

"Mallory..."

"What's she like?" Mom continued.

"She makes me laugh. She's funny." But Amy couldn't pretend another second. "Mom, I need to come home. I miss you guys. Let me come home – "

"Stop, stop," her mother said gently. "I miss you too. So much. I really wish you could come home, but you're safe there. We need to keep you safe."

"But, Mom, please..." Amy whined.

"Honey, we're only allowed five minutes to talk. Do you really want to use it crying, or can we talk to each other?"

"I'll let you two talk," Dad said. "I love you, honey," he

finished as the extension clicked.

"Okay, okay, but will you think about bringing me home?" Amy didn't want this conversation to end yet, so she quickly acquiesced.

"I will when you can answer one question for me."

"What question?"

"Who are you?"

Even through the phone lines, Mom's question made Amy see red. What the hell? What kind of a dumbass question was that? *Amy Marie Miles, age fifteen, stupid-ass drug addict, psycho-girl mental patient. Garbage her mom threw away – that's who.* But Amy held the phone in silence.

"Honey?"

"I'm here…"

"Find the good inside, baby. When you can tell me about that, then you'll be ready to come home. So tell me about Mallory."

"She's okay."

"She was your friend a minute ago. Come on. Tell me."

"Mom, I hate this place—"

"I'm sure you do. But stop this and tell me what's going on. Can't you do that?"

Amy opened her mouth to complain one more time when Ms. Avery came up. "Time's up," she said as she poised her finger over the switch hook. Then she mouthed the words, "Say goodbye now."

"Mom, I gotta go…"

"Okay, honey, I'll call again soon. I love you."

"I love you too."

Then the line went dead. Ms. Avery didn't press the switch hook until Amy heard the click on the other end. The sound was so final and Amy just broke down.

* * * *

"What kind of a stupid question was that?" Amy's voice was high-pitched and fast as she discussed her phone conversation with Ms. Prudy.

"You tell me." Ms. Prudy threw it back to Amy in her usual frustrating way. If therapists were so freakin' educated and helpful, why couldn't they answer a simple question?

"I don't know—"

"I think you do…"

"I *don't!*"

"Your mother thought you did. Or, at least, your mother thought you had the ability to find out."

"My mother's a bitch!" The second she said it, Amy was sorry.

"Is she?"

"No, no. I didn't mean that…"

"Then why'd you say it?"

"Because I was mad…"

"And that gives you the right to call people names and try to hurt them?" This conversation was not going in any direction Amy wanted it to go.

"That's not what I'm talking about…"

"I know. You want a simple answer to your question. I get that. But this brings up a bigger issue with you, Amy. What makes you think you have the right to lash out at people you care about every time you get angry or frustrated? Because I think you're actually frustrated that your mom has asked you for something you don't think you have the ability to give—an answer to the question. But rather than work on that problem, you make another by calling your mom names and getting into a fight with her even though she isn't even here."

"What she's asking is stupid—"

"Maybe, but it's somehow pushed your buttons. So maybe you need to think about it." Abruptly, Ms. Prudy got up, showed Amy the door and said, "I'll see you next time."

Chapter Twenty

Green Acres was big on physical fitness. 'Healthy body —
healthy mind' was their motto. But laps around the gym
were about to drive Amy certifiable — oh, wait, she was
already certifiably crazy — but that didn't change the fact
that if she had to walk another lap she'd scream. So she was
ecstatic when somebody came in with a Flamin' Hot Salsa
workout DVD.

"Line up, girls!" called Ms. Pearl, trying to get everyone
to settle down. *Gosh*, thought Amy, *like those captive monkeys
in the zoo, we all chatter and get excited over the least little thing*.
But it was true. With the anticipation of dancing again,
Amy could feel her palms sweat and her heart flutter in
eager excitement. She stepped up front so that she could
more easily see the monitor and the girls could see her.

The first track was a slow warm-up. Amy began to move
her shoulders then her hips while the rhythm of the drums
pounded like blood through her veins. Oh yes, oh yes,
her body seemed to relax into the familiar movement and
her muscles slipped into old patterns that felt healthy and
calming and natural. As her breath began to quicken and her
pulse stepped up a beat, Amy sucked in the old satisfaction
of music and movement. Her senses dropped to the interior
of her body as she closed her eyes and tracked the smooth
ebb and flow of her pelvis and the soft scrape of the ball of
her foot on the floor. A smile crept up from her soul to light
across her limbs and shine out of her palms.

The second track started heating things up. The beat
kicked it up a notch and instead of in-your-place stretching
and swaying, foot movements were added to dance the

girls across the floor. Amy stepped out for a grapevine to her right, but her foot stumbled. *Must be the floor.* But when the step was repeated to the left, she was awkward again. *Well, it's been a while.* But as she continued to move with the music, her body did not respond in its usual, effortless way. Amy opened her eyes and concentrated on the monitor. These were not difficult moves. Fast, yes. But not hard. "Just focus," she told herself. But it didn't matter. She was clumsy and awkward and couldn't anticipate the steps like she usually did. She had to think. No, really think. And despite commanding her feet or arms to move in the familiar patterns, some limb, some foot, was always just a little off.

* * * *

"I can't dance!" she yelled at Ms. Prudy the second the door closed for an emergency session.

"Slow down." Ms. Prudy gestured toward the chair and touched Amy's shoulder to help her settle in. "Now take a breath. No, really. Take a breath. Better. Blow it out… Slowly… Good. Now tell me."

When Amy had finished relating her stumbling attempts in the gym, Ms. Prudy sat in silence for a second. Her downcast eyes made Amy want to jump out of the chair and shake her.

"Well?" Amy asked, leaning deeply forward.

"It's not surprising, Amy," she began quietly. "That loss of coordination is one of the side effects of both Ecstasy and inhalant use. And let's face it, you used a lot. Those chemicals poison certain circuitry in the brain and keep the synapses from firing properly."

"What!" Amy couldn't help it, she jumped out of the chair. "I fried my brain and can't dance anymore?"

"Amy…"

"No! No! Why don't you just shoot me?" Forget the G-A Way. Great sobs shot out of Amy's chest before she could even finish her sentence. Not dance? *Not dance?* How could that—

"Amy, Amy," Ms. Prudy's voice was calm and soothing. "This is not set in stone. The brain is a very elastic and malleable organ. You can retrain it to respond nearly as well as it did before."

"Nearly? Nearly? What are you saying? The damage is permanent? Don't talk to me that way! You hear me? Don't say that to me!" Amy had grabbed onto Ms. Prudy's bookcase and was swaying back and forth as the words exploded out of her. With her back to Prudy, she hoped that her rage and pain were not too visible to her therapist. Amy had never wanted to show Ms. Prudy the raw side of her...but this was dance and...and...and... Oh God, this was dance.

For the next thirty minutes, Ms. Prudy talked about cross-crawl exercises, dedicated practice and brain retraining. She lectured on about returning soldiers suffering from traumatic brain injuries, relearning basic skills and other parts of the brain picking up the tasks of the damaged sections. Her words swept over Amy like soft waves of water over a dying fish, gently rocking, holding afloat, but inevitably doing nothing to change the outcome of events.

That night, Amy buried her head into her pillow and softly sobbed herself to sleep.

* * * *

Dear Diary,
I can't dance.
I can't dance.
I can't dance.
What else can I say? I can't dance. Ms. Nash asked me to write a poem about it in English class when she saw me crying at my desk. Here it is.

I am a dragonfly caught in a spider's web.
Once so iridescent, flying in an aerial ballet,

Now, paralyzed, bound and waiting to die
In a web not of my making.

What I didn't tell Ms. Nash is that this dragonfly WANTS to die.
Amy

Chapter Twenty-One

School was a joke. Amy couldn't believe what passed for academics at Green Acres. With no computers, pens, rulers, scissors, compasses, staples or textbooks allowed for fear that the inmates, ahem, *students* might use them to hurt themselves, it was damned hard to do anything in class. Teachers read to sleeping students and half-ass reports were submitted in response — written in pencil or crayon depending on the status of each girl. Since no spellcheck or thick dictionaries were allowed, writing looked like the work of a gifted kindergartener and spelling an approximation of the words for all but the most anal students.

But what they lacked in quality, they made up for in quantity. Because this was, in fact, prison, there were no summer breaks, or spring, or Christmas or Thanksgiving or…whatever. There were no holidays — just hell days. They said it was so that students could catch up on missing credits, but everyone knew it was just to torture the girls and keep them in line. In addition to a full load of academic classes, students also had to journal every day, plus attend a group processing session and take some 'issue class', as they called them.

Ironically, Amy loved her issue class. Mr. Adams was a cool, laid-back guy who taught the chemical dependency class as if he had once dealt with those issues himself. Mr. Adams was so nonjudgmental and funny that Amy felt like she could confess anything to him.

Except now.

Now, in front of her, was a drug-use tally sheet. In one column she was to list all the drugs she'd every used and how much, in the next, what it had cost her in terms of school, family, friends, health and her social life. In the last column, the truth about how she felt about each of those losses and what she was prepared to do about it.

And that's where the problem came in. For if she was honest with herself, she *liked* drugs. She didn't like what they were doing to her life, but the drugs themselves? Well, that was another story. She wanted to write that down. To actually say it out loud. If anyone would understand it, Mr. Adams would.

But what if he didn't? What if he lost his respect for her because she didn't want to change the way he hoped she would? He was, after all, teaching the CD class, as they called chemical dependency. Amy guessed that by teaching it, Adams was making some statement about how he felt about drug use—ex-user or not.

Amy started filling in the first column of the questionnaire. Pot, X, assorted inhalants, pills and… How do you write 'Anything anybody would give me'? she wondered. She began checking off the boxes on the list in the second column—

Lost friendships
Fights with friends
Fights with teachers
Fights with parents
Skipped classes
Failed classes
Might not graduate
Disrespected people I cared about
Stole from friends and family
In trouble with the law
Physically hurt people I care about
Became sexually active
Abused myself and others
Withdrew from non-using friends and family
Stopped doing activities that give me joy or I'm good at

Amy put her pencil down. The list was only half finished and yet...look...just look. Amy's palms had become damp with perspiration. So had her brow. She reached up to brush her hair back and erase the tiny droplets on her face, but she could not erase the facts staring her in the face. She liked drugs. She liked the escape they gave her. She liked that they were cool drugs — not crazy-people meds. She liked to feel in control. Yet the list was there and growing before her eyes. The people she'd hurt. The damage she'd done. The love and joy she'd given up. She'd known it had cost her... but this much? Amy's hand was shaking as she reached over to close the page and hide the list from her eyes.

"You okay, Amy?" Mr. Adams had only touched the back of her chair as he spoke, but Amy knew it was his way of comforting her.

"Fine, fine," Amy said, trying to straighten herself up.

"It's okay," Mr. Adams continued. "This is often a startling activity for students. There's something about seeing it all in black and white — "

"That's it!" whispered Amy as she noticed a head or two look up from their papers. "I knew drugs were causing me some problems...but...but...not this." Even to herself, Amy could recognize the despondency in her voice. But she didn't even want to cry. This sorrow was deeper than that. She needed to be alone.

"Class, let's come into a circle," Mr. Adams instructed.

The last thing Amy wanted to do was process with the class. She didn't want to hear what they had to say and she certainly didn't want to share, but here she was, stuck in the middle of her own Ring Around the Rosie, just waiting until she could fall down.

"Does anyone have any feelings about this activity that they would like to share?" began Mr. Adams.

Sam sat up tall in her chair to answer. A tall, quiet gay transgender with slicked-back hair and chiseled features, Sam was on level Conclude and was chairing the CD class as part of her get-out-of-jail final responsibilities. She — or he, as Sam preferred to be called — had a confidence about him that Amy secretly admired. While Kelly and Andrea snickered at his slim build in boy clothes, Amy believed that Sam might just be the one to keep it all together when he got out of Green Acres.

"You all know that I was a cutter and a huffer before I came here. I felt like I needed a way to escape the torture of being in the wrong body, the bullying, the ridicule... Just everything. I watched my boyfriend have a full-blown seizure in an alley where we were huffing. Nobody was around and by the time I got help *he* wasn't there anymore. He lives with his mom now and she takes care of him. He can't talk, or walk. His mom feeds him. He doesn't even know who I am. And he has to wear diapers..." Sam dropped his head and traced the lines on his hand with his index finger before looking back up. "Diapers."

The girls all sat locked in their own thoughts. Somebody coughed, a couple of girls shifted in their seats.

"I loved everybody when I was on X," began Jordan. "It was the one thing that could relieve my need to cut. And when I say everybody, I mean everybody. I slept with three guys at one party just because I felt so good...so much love...so much...I don't know... You know?"

"How did that make you feel?" asked Mr. Adams.

"Fine, I thought," Jordan said, shrugging. "I mean, I said it was no big deal. Consenting adults — well, not really adults — but consenting, you know? But then, whenever I was alone or quiet, it would just pop into my head again and I'd need to vent. And then it just kept popping in more and more and I'd vent more and more. My shrink said that all the scars on my arm mean that it's not fine..."

As Jordan's voice trailed off, one quiet voice, then another filled the center of the circle.

"I hit my mom."

"I called my best friend a slut and now she won't speak to me again."

"I stole the rent money from my mom's purse."

"I took the car and hit a guardrail."

"Girls, girls, one at a time—" Mr. Adams tried to break in, but the confessions were coming as if conjured up by some magic potion.

"I slept with my sister's boyfriend."

"I shoplifted from the game shop even though they gave me discounts all the time."

And in the middle of it, Amy felt like she was in church, although it was like no church she'd ever been in before. The raw honesty swept aside any negative judgments or feelings of 'I'm better than...' and in their place was an acceptance and deep love of each of these girls—and herself—that she had never known was possible.

"I fried my brain with E and inhalants, and... I can't dance anymore," she shared. And at that moment her losses— all her losses—were clear. The cost was evident. And the illusion of any benefit was shattered.

This was followed by another girl's confession, and another's.

"I failed my chemistry exam 'cause I was high and lost my scholarship."

"I knocked a hole in my wall."

"I pushed my little sister on the ground."

No one cared who spoke or who answered, and Mr. Adams suddenly became quiet and let the girls speak their most painful truths over and over. Each voice was barely above a whisper and yet the stories seemed to fill the entire room. Even when the bell rang, the confessions continued and Mr. Adams allowed the agony to escape in its slow, sacred flow until that flow settled to a trickle and finally stopped.

"You've taken the first major step here, ladies..." he said softly. "These confessions are not fodder for gossip. Accept these truths as a sacred gift from your fellow travelers on this difficult journey and hold them in silence until we meet again." Then he touched his palms together in front of his heart and said, "I acknowledge your deep bravery as you step out into the world today. It is my profound honor to know you all and walk with you on this journey."

With that, he made a small sweeping gesture with his hand and invited the girls to leave class. Every girl walked out in silence.

* * * *

(After class today, I just have to come back and write about this poem again.)

Dear Diary,
I can't dance.
I can't dance.
I can't dance.
What else can I say? I can't dance. Ms. Nash asked me to write a poem about it in English class when she saw me crying at my desk. Here it is.

I am a dragonfly caught in a spider's web.
Once so iridescent, flying in an aerial ballet,
Now, paralyzed, bound and waiting to die
In a web not of OF my making. (OMG, I did do this. I DID. Shit.)

What I didn't tell Ms. Nash is that this dragonfly WANTS to die.
Amy

Class today was gnarly. I told Ms. Prudy and they put me on the biofeedback game again. I keep doing it, but never could get that stupid balloon to float evenly – except today, I did. I just kept thinking about what was said in class and it really made me sad. But the thing about the game is that you can't think of anything except breathing. I don't know why it felt good to launch that balloon across the ravine – but it did.

Chapter Twenty-Two

The Commit team had earned an outing and Amy was thrilled. Cabin fever had infected everyone in the dorm and the girls were at one another's throats. Funny, at home loneliness had so often been Amy's problem. Now? What she would do for a little alone time.

"Don't forget the bug spray! You need bug spray!" Emily happily chased after Mallory with a plastic spray bottle. Clearly, it was not full of bug spray, as chemicals like that were strictly forbidden. But Amy couldn't stop watching as one might watch a train wreck, for everyone knew you just didn't invade Mallory's personal space like that.

Like a tiger, Mallory quickly checked the territory then sprang. She grabbed Emily by the front of her shirt, getting in real close. Her words were so quiet and slow, they silenced the room as both Amy and Mia stood watching. "Don't. You. Ever. Spray. Me. With. Anything. Again. You. Dingbat."

Emily's cheery grin instantly melted into a pouting puddle as tears sprang up in her eyes. Mallory let go and brushed down the front of Emily's shirt. "Okay, okay," she softened. "I know you didn't mean to piss me off. But you can't do that to people. Get it?"

Emily bobbed her head in clear relief and Mallory crossed the room to get her shoes. "Are we supposed to wear these things?" she asked, picking up the pull-on slippers they were allowed in the building.

"No," Emily offered with her usual excitement at knowing an answer. "They have our hiking shoes locked up. We're supposed to go up in our socks and they'll check the shoes out to us just before we leave."

"Then let's leave," smiled Mallory, reaching over to loop her arm into Emily's. Amy turned in time to see Emily drop her head and hide the smile that threatened to spill right past the frame of her face.

With bottles of water and good athletic shoes, the girls hiked deep into the woods for which Green Acres got its name. The path undulated under old-growth laurel and oak dotted with hostas, ferns and a thick carpet of decaying leaves. Huge white granite boulders formed stark contrast to the deep greens and browns of the woods, and sunlight played hide-and-seek with hikers as they slipped from the dark shade of the canopy to the vibrant blue of the open sky.

"Ladies, there will be no talking for the first mile of the hike," Ms. Brookes announced as they stood at the mouth of the path. "This is not a punishment, but instead a way to let you focus on the sounds of nature and a chance to get out of your head. Listen. Just listen. Seriously. I'll let you know when you can talk."

In the beginning Amy and Mallory couldn't help but 'talk'. Their sophisticated sign language allowed them to make wisecracks about Emily's walk, or Mia's focused gaze or Kelly's aggressive pace. But as they wandered farther into the woods, the sounds of their surroundings started to compel their attention.

When a leaf blew across Amy's face, she brushed it away and became aware of both the feel and sound of the soft breeze that carried the leaf. Walking along, she began to focus on the constant swishing of that breeze through the trees as it contrasted with the higher, more insistent humming of the myriad insects that flew around their feet and legs as they stepped along the leaf-carpeted path.

The girls rounded the bend behind a rock outcrop — several beams of sunlight shot orange through the leaves and lit the ground in front of them. Amy's heart leaped into her throat. Her mom had so often told her that those beams were God talking to her. She had always brushed off her mom's remarks as silly old-fashioned nonsense. Besides, Amy didn't believe in God. God sure didn't believe in her, or he wouldn't have given her lousy bipolar disorder and all the grief that went with it. But here, walking in silence amidst this living, singing forest, she could feel her mom's words—and even feel her mom. And…maybe…God? Just then a jay swooped over the girls' heads, cawing and dive-bombing, and their silence was broken by squeals and peals of surprised laughter.

"Girls." Ms. Brooke held a finger to her lips and signaled the girls ahead. But the truth was that she didn't really need to hush them, the woods had already grabbed their attention.

Amy thought back to those sunbeams as she continued trudging up the slope. She couldn't remember the last time she'd seen anything like that. Actually, she couldn't remember the last time she'd *seen* anything. As she took in the waxy emerald green of the mountain laurel or the lacy grace of the ferns lining the path, Amy was surprised at this moment of comfort within herself. She realized she hated to be alone, or still, or quiet, because she was afraid of what she'd find inside if she was left alone with 'her'. But here she was. Silent. Not distracted. Totally alone with her thoughts.

And it was okay. It was okay.

Scenes of J-J, Stacey, little things, not so little things, floated across her mind. But it was like they weren't part of her…just disembodied images that floated in and floated out. In the middle of her thoughts the sharp buzz of a ruby-throated hummingbird startled her as the bird buzzed right up to her face then hovered just inches from her nose, staring eyeball to eyeball. Amy caught her breath and stood motionlessly, gaping back, a small smile growing into a giant grin as she stared face to face with this beautiful, wondrous creature. Then, just as quickly as it had come it darted off and disappeared.

Mallory's eyes grew as big as plates as she mouthed, "Could you believe that!" to Amy's astonished face. It was all Amy could do to hold in the well of laughter that threatened to break the silence of the woods and echo down the canyon.

Chapter Twenty-Three

Mail. It was mail. For her. From her mother.

Amy ripped the envelope open. Her mom had finally, finally replied to her letters. She was out of here. Reprieved. Gone. Free.

She knew her mother had said no on the phone and had ignored all her previous letters, but Amy hadn't been able to really tell her how things were because the phones were so public and her earlier letters were brief. So she'd sent a long letter telling her mom everything. Once her mom really knew how things were, Amy was sure she'd acquiesce and see the light. Amy had been thinking about her actions before coming to G-A and, while they weren't the best, her behavior was fixable — really, had already been fixed — so Amy was sure that, with a good explanation, her mom would agree to give it a try and let her come home.

It was their few minutes of free time and Amy was reading on her bed when Ms. Brooke came by with the letter. Amy rubbed the outside of the envelope with her palms, feeling the small indentations from her mom's pen. Then she put the envelope to her nose. Sure enough, it had just the faintest smell of home still clinging to the paper. Amy scrunched up her pillow, scooted back into its soft cushion and settled in to read.

My Darling Amy,

I'm so sorry that you are having such a hard time adjusting. Remember, though, they told us it would be difficult. That's the problem with any real change. First you have to dislodge all the old habits, and they don't want to go. So sometimes you have to bulldoze them out, and that kind of self-excavation hurts. But once that's done, you can begin to rebuild your life and your future.

It breaks my heart to hear you're so sad, but I have faith that you can succeed in changing your life. You are a remarkable young lady with unlimited potential and I am so excited to watch the changes that I know will happen in you.

I love you dearly, my daughter, and I miss you more than words can say. I wish that our journey could be side by side along this path, but that can't be. You must find your own truth alone on your quest, and I must find mine so I can be ready when you come back to us.

Be brave. Know that we are with you in spirit and keep moving forward until you find your truth.

I love you,
Mom

What kind of crap was that? Amy rolled onto her stomach on the bed and dropped her head into the pillow so her roommates couldn't see her tears. *Alone on your quest? Find your own truth? You've got to be freakin' kidding me! 'I'll come get you' – that would be more like it. I miss you more than words can say? What bullshit. If you miss me, come get me.*

Lost in her pain, Amy changed, finished her night toiletry and climbed into bed just before lights out. But sleep eluded her. As she fell into the netherland between wake and sleep, she saw herself, arm outstretched, standing on the platform of a train as it began leaving the station. Her mother was there, her fingers gently brushing against Amy's but lower, reaching up from her position on the ground below the train. As the train pulled away, Amy desperately reached out to continue feeling her mother's touch. She felt the railing of the guardrail dig into her waist as she struggled to keep contact. Her shoulder ached as she stretched her arm socket as far as it could go. But the train kept moving and her mother's touch fell farther and farther back. As Amy began to cry, her mother just stood there—never running, never trying to reach her, but there, frozen on the platform, letting her daughter go.

Her anguish turned to soft cries at the pain of such loss as other, quietly aching cries crept into her dream…and into her consciousness.

With her eyes still closed, Amy's drift into the realm of sleep was disrupted by the mournful whimpers of Mia in the bottom bunk. Through closed eyelids Amy sensed that the room was still dark and the night still new. Threatening hisses and small, animal-like gasps emanated from Mia's bed. Shuffling sounds, fierce staccato whispers and tiny cries filled the air with tension and urgency.

Just as darkness can clear as the eyes become accustomed to the blackness, so too Amy's ears became acutely aware of each minute sound coming from Mia's bed. Kelly was there. And not invited as a friend or lover, but rather intruding as a threat. *So that was what had terrified Mia.* Her mind raced back to the dropped note, the trampled fingers, the anguished screams of the fragile little girl when confronted by the bully that was Kelly. *Should I stop it? Could I help? Oh God.* Kelly was huge and mean and ruthless. *Do I want to be her next victim?* But how could she leave Mia to the assault when she knew — *knew* — that Mia was getting hurt? What could she —

"Enough! Get up *now!*" As she bolted into an upright position, Amy would have never believed that the same Ms. Pearl who had so gently helped her through her first body check could erupt with such demanding rage, but there she stood at the door, and, looking at her, Amy could have sworn Pearl had grown six inches taller.

"E ticket offense, backup in Room 3!" In one swift movement, Ms. Pearl flipped on the light, called for backup on the intercom and scooped Mia out from under the grip of Kelly, who sat half naked on the bed, wearing a cold-blooded threat on her face. Instantly Ms. Brooke and a male attendant came in and grabbed the defiant Kelly by each arm. As she squirmed and swore, they escorted her toward Isolation as Ms. Pearl shouted orders in an astonishingly controlled voice.

"Keep fighting, Kelly, and you'll stay for two rounds. Settle down and you'll be out in two hours. Decide. You know how much you hate it."

Clearly this was not the first time that Kelly had been carted off to the Isolation Room, and her howls and curses seemed to indicate that a short stay was not in the offing. Yet for Amy, the stay could not be long enough. The energy of Kelly's savagery still hung in the room. Amy suddenly had to pee but didn't know if she was capable of walking to the toilet.

"Show's over, girls. Go back to sleep." Ms. Pearl still had the no-nonsense cadence that had surprised Amy before and she decided she'd hold it rather than risk Ms. Pearl's tone. With Mia still in tow, Ms. Pearl turned off the light and slipped out of the door, leaving Amy, Mallory and Emily in stunned silence.

"It's about time," Mallory whispered when Pearl's footsteps had faded down the hall.

"Well, at least we don't have to worry for a while," Emily added in her usual, inappropriately cheerful tone.

"You mean, you knew?" asked Amy, astonished that such brutality might be happening under her nose and no one was doing anything about it.

"Everyone knew," Mallory answered.

"Why didn't you *do* anything about it?" Amy couldn't stop the question before it popped out—she was appalled that her friend would look the other way, but at the same time ashamed that she too had listened and feared to act.

"What?"

"I mean…"

"Listen, bitch…" Mallory's tone sent a shock wave over to Amy. How could her friend talk to her that way? "Kelly plays for keeps. She has no problem beating the crap outta you—she'd kill you if she could. Don't be judging things you freakin' don't understand. I don't need that self-righteous crap from you. Do you hear me, bitch?"

"I hear you…" Amy's voice was soft and small. She had no intention of engaging in any kind of confrontation with Mallory, and was terrified of what this exchange would do to their friendship.

"Now go to freakin' sleep," Mallory ordered.

Amy turned to the wall and pulled the blanket over her shoulder. But she could not sleep. In fact, she didn't know if she ever would again.

Chapter Twenty-Four

Buzz! Buzz! Buzz!

Amy was sure she could live at Green Acres for the rest of her life and her heart would still hit the ceiling every time that morning buzzer sounded. She slapped her bed together, making sure that the hospital corners were neat and that the fold under the pillow was tucked in tight. So it wasn't until she slid down from her top bunk that she realized that neither Mia nor Mallory was in the room.

"Okay, girls," said Ms. Pearl, sticking her head quickly in the door. Clearly, since she didn't raise an eyebrow at the empty beds, their absence was expected. Amy figured that Mia would be in the Infirmary, but she couldn't make out where Mallory would have gone, or why.

"Emily," she began, knowing that getting any real information from Emily's la-la-land was basically impossible, "did you hear Mallory leave last night?"

"No," sang Emily as she did her little foot-dance toward the bathroom. "I guess she had one of her spells again. She has depression, you know. Maybe it's a blue day."

With that, she danced herself right into the bathroom.

Wow. Amy hadn't seen any signs of depression. And you'd think she'd catch that since she was practically the queen of fall-into-your-grave sadness. *You just never know.*

Amy went through the motions of chores and school, but by the afternoon, she was getting genuinely worried about Mallory. She confided in Ms. Pearl, who gave her permission to visit Mallory in the Infirmary, but Amy was unprepared for what she found.

If she had been lying in her casket, Mallory's eyes could

not have looked more dead. With her gaze fixed at the ceiling, Mallory lay motionless and silent. Her freckles stood out on her skin, which no longer held its usual rich, warm brown hue, but now was gray-toned and flat. She didn't even glance over when Amy walked in the door.

"You had me scared, Mal."

Nothing.

"Was it something I said or did?" Mallory's violent reaction to the Mia situation was still heavily on Amy's mind and she hoped that it wasn't the root of this depression. But if she wasn't guilty, Amy prayed that this wide-open invitation would encourage one of Mallory's famous wisecracks and she would snap out of it.

But there was no response.

"What's going on, Mal? I've never seen you this way." Amy touched her friend's arm as she leaned in. Mallory's eyes slowly drifted to Amy's face, stopping short of her eyes before lingering for a moment and slowly closing. She never said a word.

Amy felt like she had been dismissed. She was hurt. No, confused. Or…maybe angry? *What do I feel? One second we're soulmates, the next I'm totally locked out. I get she's depressed. I know depressed. Well, maybe not like this. No, not like this.* Maybe that was the problem. This isolation and shutting out. When Amy was depressed she sought to involve people in her pain. She often got angry and wanted everyone else to feel as awful as she did. But this? This was something she didn't understand. It made her feel helpless and that made her angry.

Back in her room, Amy started folding her clothes and putting her things away. What had caused Mallory's meltdown? Was it her? Was it Kelly? No, she decided, it was *her* fault. It was her fault that she'd questioned her friend when she didn't know how bad Kelly was. But how could she? Who'd have thought that somebody could savage another person the way Kelly had tormented Mia? She was just a little white girl from the suburbs. Ha! Amy had to laugh. She'd always thought she was so tough. She'd always been so sure of herself at home. Thought she was streetwise. But here? Here the rules were all new to her. She didn't feel like she could find her footing. As much as she broke the rules at home, she realized how sheltered she really was. How her protected suburban life was really a joke here. Was Mallory right? Would Kelly kill somebody? Amy didn't know. And she hated not knowing. It gnawed at her like dog teeth on bone — grating, chipping, agitating. And that uncertainty filled her chest with a tightness that gripped down hard and raised her blood pressure. She felt the pressure move into her face. Into her hands. She felt the heat rise from her solar plexus to her throat until it rushed out like a shot from her hand and her arm swept all her belongings off her top shelf and onto the floor. Her thoughts raced by in seconds and were finished before her stuff could even hit the floor. Her things struck against the concrete with such a satisfying crack that she reached over to Mallory's shelf and did it again. *Yes, yes.* "For you, Mallory!" she yelled as brushes, toothpaste, shampoo and family pictures crashed everywhere. The tightness in her chest exploded out, leaving her the ability to breathe...and sit.

So she sat. She just sat.

Within seconds Ms. Pearl and Ms. Avery were in the room. Clearly ready to pounce and drop her to the ground, the two women stopped at the door as if restricted by a gate.

"What was that all about?" asked Ms. Avery, clearly irritated.

"I got stressed...ma'am." Amy's voice was quiet as she sat on the floor.

"No kidding."

"No kidding," came Amy's soft retort.

Ms. Pearl opened her mouth to speak when Avery held up one hand and pointed to herself with the other. Pearl turned and left.

"That's a D ticket—destroying property. Clean it up and report to me for detention chores."

"Yes, ma'am."

"That's it? That's all you've got to say about this mess?"

"Uh-huh."

"You know, Amy, I don't like your attitude. You may have everyone else fooled into thinking that you're following the rules and making improvements, but I know better. I think you're a kiss-ass who knows how to scam the system. I think that you'd better get off your high horse and really dig into the G-A Way. I think you've got a lot of crap going on that you're just not willing to deal with and you need to get on it or you're never going to make the kinds of changes that you need to succeed outside these walls."

Avery seemed to have slowed down and lost her wind when she started back up again.

"Let's just see if we can take you down a notch or two."

"Didn't you just do that...?" Amy let a long pause hang in the air with her mouth still forming the end of her 't' until she quietly added "...ma'am."

"And another A ticket for rudeness."

Amy kept her eyes even and her mouth closed as she stared at Avery. She said and did nothing that would allow the woman to reprimand her, but she never dropped her eyes or signaled surrender. Finally Avery turned to leave.

"Have that all picked up in five minutes or I'll cite you again." She threw the threat over her shoulder as she walked away. The heaviness of her step made Amy smile.

Then she reached down and began replacing her belongings onto the shelf.

* * * *

Dear Diary,

I'm alone. I'm freakin' alone!

Mallory's gone into her own world. I get she's depressed, but I need her. Why can't she snap out of it and we'll do this together? I hate that she's pulled away from me. Left me. I need her and she's abandoned me. I hate depression – it's such a selfish disease. All about them. Doesn't she get that friends don't do that to friends? I need her.

I love her.

Amy

Chapter Twenty-Five

Under different circumstances, cleaning the bathroom sinks with a toothbrush might be a really disgusting and demoralizing task. But like everything else, the sinks at Green Acres were cleaned so thoroughly and regularly by the resident girls that Amy really didn't mind the punishment. Besides, it got her out of PE and walking endless laps of the room without Mallory, so all in all, it was fine. In fact, she had finished nine out of ten sinks when a light slap on her butt made her look up.

"So, dumb shit, what got you Bitch Brush?" The half-dead Mallory from the day before was gone, replaced by the girl Amy had thought she'd known all along.

"I cleared our bedroom shelves," answered Amy. She continued to concentrate on scouring the last sink and didn't look up. As she scrubbed, she tried to make the pieces of her life with Mallory fit together.

"No shit?" Mallory said, a smile in her voice. "So, our Little Goody Two-Shoes came out of her shell?"

"I suppose." Amy still couldn't look up at her friend.

"When will you be done here?" Mallory was talking as if nothing had happened. She was just picking up as if... as if...

"Mal, why didn't you tell me about your depression?" Amy just couldn't pretend that the day before hadn't happened.

"What about it?"

"You were scary."

"I don't want to talk about it."

"But I do." Amy needed to know. "Was it my fault? Did I

say something? Did I—"

"Why does everything have to be about you, Amy?" Mallory's good mood was gone and she'd stepped right up to Amy. "I was depressed, all right? I get depressed sometimes. It's no big deal and really not your business. Who died and named you shrink? I don't want to talk about it…and especially not with you. Be my friend. Don't be my friend. But mind your own freakin' business." Mallory had turned to leave the bathroom when Amy caught her arm, feeling the taut muscles under her hand.

"Wait. I'm sorry." She felt just awful for upsetting Mallory like this. "You're right, it's not my business. I'm sorry."

"Fine. Fine." Mallory's voice was low as her body released its tension and her arm relaxed into Amy's grip. She did a little playful wobble and leaned into Amy's side. "So, you done yet? You done?"

"Yeah, I'm done." Amy couldn't help smiling—the familiar Mallory had returned and was asking her to play. "Let me just get Avery to check this off."

"So hurry up and we'll catch the end of PE—they're doing Hot Salsa," Mallory said as she pulled Amy's arm toward the gym where Ms. Avery would be supervising.

"Hot Salsa?" groaned Amy. "I don't want to do that. Let's just hang in the bathroom, I'll pretend I'm not done yet."

"No, no. It's fun. So much less boring than walking laps."

"I don't want to."

"Why not?"

"'Cause."

"'Cause why?"

"Come on, Mal. I just don't, okay?"

"Whatever. I'm goin'. Come if you want. Don't come. Who cares? But I'm not sitting around in the john watching you scrub sinks." And with that, Mallory turned and walked into the gym, leaving Amy standing alone in the hall with her toothbrush.

* * * *

131

"So why didn't you go to dance?" Of course Ms. Prudy would not let that pass when Amy really wanted to talk about her deteriorating relationship with Mallory.

"That's not important," began Amy. "It's that Mal abandoned me."

"No, it's that you abandoned yourself — your talents and passions. And *you* abandoned your friend in the process."

"That's not how it happened." Amy pulled her knees up to her chin as she began to press her case with Ms. Prudy.

"I think that's exactly how it happened, Amy. Mallory approached you in friendship, asked you to reconnect with her through the playfulness of dance, and you let your fears get the best of you and rejected both the opportunity to dance and the opportunity to bond with your friend."

"You've twisted it all around!" Amy scratched her fingertips across her knees, gritting her teeth as she stared at Ms. Prudy.

"How so?" Prudy's voice was calm and quiet as she looked right back at Amy.

"She should have stayed with me — "

"Hiding in the bathroom?"

"Well, yes…"

"So how are either of you going to get well if you hide in the bathroom and never face your fears? Is that where you want to spend the rest of your life — living in hiding in the midst of crap? Is that really what you want for yourself?"

"But I can't dance anymore…"

"And that's the real problem, isn't it?"

Amy could only nod. Tears closed her throat to words.

"So what are you going to do about it?"

Amy's head shot up and droplets of spit flung from her mouth as the tears and pain of her answer exploded. "What can I do?"

"Practice."

"That's easy for you to say. You don't get it."

"What don't I get?"

"My feet don't listen anymore. My body doesn't feel it…"

"I get it. I really do, Amy. Something that was once so easy — so natural — isn't anymore. Okay. That's gone. That's the price you paid for the drugs you used. There's nothing you can do about that. Your only question now is — is it gone forever or are you going to fight to get back something you love? All the other regret, self-pity and longing are useless wastes of your energy. This isn't the last thing that's going to be hard in your life. But how full or miserable your life is going to be will be determined by how you handle the hard things in life. Fight for your dreams, and you'll have a rich life. Run, and you may as well just set up shop in the toilet. It's up to you."

Amy's face was wet with tears, but beneath the dampness she felt herself harden under Ms. Prudy's words. This was *not* her fault. This was *not* some character test. This was dance. She couldn't do it. And she had a right to be sad.

* * * *

Dear Diary,

Mallory got mad at me today.

I didn't want to go to dance because…well, you know why. Mal threw a fit afterward and told me to grow up. I started to get pissed back and fight with her, but then she said something. Let's see if I can get this right. She said,

"Amy, you are one of the most amazing people I know. You have so much to give. But you hide it with so much shit most people can't see it. Crawl out from under that pile, hose yourself off and be brilliant. Wouldn't it piss everyone off if you actually lived up to your potential? God, girl, you could change the world."

Can you believe she said that to me? I hit her in the shoulder and she threw me on the bed. I still didn't go to dance. But I'm thinking about it.

Amy

Chapter Twenty-Six

Mia came back the next day. Usually when there were problems in a particular dorm the girls were separated into different rooms, but staff always seemed to make an exception with Mia. Mallory and Amy were actually glad that she came back. Quiet and neat with the ability to keep to herself, she was the least intrusive roommate anyone could have. Emily, of course, was thrilled to have her 'family' back together again and, after an extra-sloppy, extra-long welcome back hug, went skipping out of the room to tell anyone who'd listen that Mia was back.

"You okay?" Mallory asked as Mia put her clothes back into her drawer.

Mia slowly bobbed her head but tears began to form at her lids.

"Can we do anything, Mia?" Amy sincerely wanted to be able to relieve this girl's constant pain—if not for Mia, for herself. Mia's invariable sorrow reminded Amy of her own homesickness and feelings of loss. Mallory had been right when she described Mia as a wet blanket—she always threw a veil of sorrow over everything around her.

"I'm okay," ventured Mia in a small voice.

"Did you hear they sent Kelly to juvie?" Mallory offered this information as a gift to Mia.

"Really?" Amy was surprised. "I thought she was still in Isolation."

"No way," continued Mallory, as she smiled and motioned the girls closer. "She threw a real knock-down, drag-out in Isolation—caught Mr. Joe in the mouth and knocked out a tooth. That was it. They decided, what with

Mia and everything, she was too dangerous to ever come back here again. She'll be in the psych ward at juvie, but, Mia—that bitch will never torment you again."

Mia's lips turned up in the smallest expression of a smile, but her eyes opened wider and seemed infused with a spark of life that Amy had never believed even existed in the girl. Apparently Mallory saw it too, for she started dancing around the room, flinging Mia's clothing like confetti as she skipped to her own rendition of that *Wizard of Oz* song—

"Ding-dong the bitch is dead
Which ol' bitch?
The Kelly bitch
Ding-dong the Kelly bitch is dead!"

It didn't matter that Mia put her hand over her mouth to try to hide it—the laugh that escaped from her was definitely worth Mallory's effort, and Mia's joy spilled over until Mallory couldn't help herself and playfully pushed the smaller girl onto her bed.

Mia instantly grabbed her pillow and threw it back at Mallory.

"Oh, so that's the way it is?" shouted Mallory in mock injury as she grabbed Mia's clothes and began pelting the squealing, giggling girl with shirts, and pants and panties. Amy grabbed Emily's water bottle and began spritzing both girls as they threw anything and everything they could get their hands on.

It didn't take a minute before Ms. Brooke ran up to the door. As Amy squirted her friends, her amusement grew as she saw Ms. Brooke stop and linger at the threshold of the door. Amy knew Ms. Brooke would have to stop the frolicking any second, but until she did, Amy intended to enjoy the moment to its fullest.

"I didn't see this," Ms. Brooke finally said, bobbing her index finger at the wet floor, scattered clothing and rumpled beds. "Have it cleaned up in five minutes and it never happened," she continued as she threw a wink over her shoulder and left the room.

As they folded clothes and wiped the floor, Amy looked over at Mia's composed face. "Welcome back, Mia," she said.

"Thank you." And a smile bloomed across Mia's face.

Chapter Twenty-Seven

Dear Stacey,

What gives, girl? I've written to you five times and you aren't writing back. You're supposed to be my best friend. Best friends write. They talk to each other. They're there when friends are in trouble.

In fact, no one has written. Not one person. It makes me feel like I have no friends back there. Do I? Please write and let me know.

How is Kairyn? Does J-J ever mention me? Have you seen Danny around?

This is so hard, Stace. They push, push, push for us to be these perfect people. They never let up. As soon as you accomplish one thing, they want you to do the next. It's like when we played limbo – no sooner do you contort yourself into a pretzel to make it under the bar, do it, and want to cheer, when they say, 'No, no, not yet... Here, let me lower that bar for you... Now, do it again.' I want to know when I can sit back and cheer.

That's why I need your letters. I need you to cheer for me.

A girl here was molested by another girl. It was so scary. But it made me think about some of the things we did. Not that we were ever as mean as this girl – no way. But I kinda like the girl who was molested. And when I saw how scared and sad she was, it makes me think about how we used people. I bet some of them felt pretty awful when we were done. Do you ever think about that, Stace? Just wondering.

I hate it here and really want to see you. I miss my old life and sometimes get scared that you are all moving on without me. Please write and tell me it's okay. 'Kay? Or just send me a picture. Whatever. I asked Mom to send you stamped envelopes last time I talked to her. She said she'd drop them in the mail. So,

please write. I miss you.
Love,
Amy

Chapter Twenty-Eight

Over the next month, Amy worked to Climb the Cs. Her goals on Commit had been attending class, completing all homework assignments, keeping her room up to standards at all times, following the G-A Way when it came to respect of staff and peers regardless of mood and pushing herself to conform to the rigors and regiment of the program.

As she progressed to Conquer, expectations were raised. Ms. Prudy was pushing her hard to overcome her reluctance to dance. She was also being pressured to step outside her comfort zone in academics, physical challenges and emotional baggage. Amy had kicked her grade point average up several notches and was pleased with As in English, earth science and humanities.

She'd also done well on the wilderness hike. She'd been given a map and a compass and had had to figure out how to get back to base camp. Luckily a random drawing had paired her with Mallory, so even when they got lost for an hour, being together was so much fun that Amy hadn't minded coming in last place.

Even the emotional stuff appeared better from the outside. Amy wasn't getting any C tickets and the occasional B was easy to work off. Amy didn't even count A tickets—a few swear words or a smart remark to staff were definitely worth the price.

Outwardly Amy was a model student. But inside, she felt it was all crap. Emily needed to stay there because her parents wouldn't have her and she clearly didn't have the sense to take care of herself. Mia couldn't get through a day without crying and would rather die than stand up for herself. Kelly — well, Kelly would need to stay locked in solitary forever for everyone's protection. But Amy? She just didn't have the same issues and really just wanted — no, *needed* — to go home.

But in the meantime, Mallory was her friend, her sister, her soulmate. Amy had never again seen the depressive meltdown Mallory had experienced before and the girls just became closer and closer. So when Mallory suggested that they cheek their meds, the plan sounded like a fun lark to Amy. Despite several changes in her cocktail, Amy still longed for the day when she could feel the full range of her emotions and not be harnessed into this straightjacket of 'normalcy'. Mallory had cleaned out her shampoo bottle and each day the girls would cheek their morning meds then stash them in the bottle. Amy had to be careful not to smile when the flashlight scanned her mouth but missed the tiny pills tucked between her molars and her cheek. Mallory had taught her the flash-quick move with her tongue that planted the pills while she pretended to swig her water. Amy admired Mallory's deadpan expression as she walked away from med check. The whole thing was a hoot.

The girls began making plans to live together when they got out of Green Acres. Amy lived right off the commuter train station and they could rent an apartment close to her house, find jobs at the local mall and use the train to commute to college when they turned eighteen. Mallory would decorate her room in African animal prints and Amy's would be sleek, modern and black. They would get a tabby cat and name it Asylum.

Their dreams were enhanced by Sam's graduation from the program. After a formal Conclusion party with soda and cake, Sam was awarded the traditional C trophy with a miniature mountain climber on top and a certificate claiming that he had successfully Climbed the Cs. He'd written a group letter a month later describing his new apartment, an intern position at a hotel in the laundry room and a new boyfriend. G-A had been atwitter for days, buzzing about Sam's new life. Now, another month later, the girls were still using Sam's success as their benchmark.

"But I wouldn't want to work in a laundry," Mallory had declared as they walked back from academics.

"It would suck," Amy agreed. "But she's—he's—getting paid *and* getting college credit at the same time."

"On second thought, I guess I might do it if it got me out of the house," Mallory offered with no particular conviction.

"Maybe," agreed Amy. "But I have other plans. I'd like to be an actress or one of those voiceover people. You know? Then you could get fat, or come to work in your jammies and still make big bucks and everyone could hear your voice." As she spoke, Amy pulled an imaginary microphone up to her lips, opened her legs into a wide stance and used her other hand for dramatic effect as she fell into her best public announcer voice. "Here are the coming attractions for movies scheduled for a theater near you!" Then, in a comical aside, she added, "Oh, and don't forget to buy that big honkin' bag of popcorn before the movie starts!"

But as much as Amy tried to entertain her friend, Mallory stayed unengaged as they walked back to their room.

There, Amy's CD homework grabbed her attention.

"Great," Amy muttered. "Have you finished your CD homework?"

"Oh crap." Mallory's answer carried none of the urgency setting into Amy's voice.

"Sit down, we still have a few minutes before CD class, let's do it."

"Noooo," whined Mallory as she threw herself on her bed. "I'm too tired. I don't care. Let's just try to distract Mr. Adams with some question. You know how he is. Get him started and we won't have to talk about homework at all."

"But I like his class—" Amy began.

"Me too, but don't be a kiss-ass. I really don't feel like doing my homework…" Mallory rolled to her side on her bed and put a pillow over her ear and eyes. Clearly the conversation was over. Amy sprawled out in the chair and closed her eyes for a minute. She didn't risk lying down as she feared she'd fall asleep and miss class altogether. She'd accept a B ticket for late homework, but she had no intention of getting a C ticket for missing class.

Minutes later, Amy's chair jerked as the edge of sleep faltered her balance and threatened to spill her right out of the seat.

"Get up! Gotta go!" she called to Mallory as she grabbed her CD workbook and headed down the hallway. It wasn't until she got to the class door that she realized Mallory hadn't followed. Going back would earn her a C ticket. She couldn't do that. With one last, hopeful look over her shoulder, Amy entered class with the other girls.

Inside, something felt weird. Everyone was quiet, or whispering among themselves.

"What's going on?" Amy asked Jordan as she found a seat.

"Sam crashed," Jordan whispered.

"Crashed?"

"'Got arrested for doing E. Lost his internship...and the guy. It all sucks."

Just then, Mr. Adams walked into the room.

"Okay, I know you heard about Sam. We need to talk. Who wants to start?"

Oh, Mal. You should be here. We're saved by the crash. No tickets will be handed out today, and there you are, stuck in your bed. But in the next instant Amy's joy at her own good fortune turned into first sadness, then fear about what Sam's crash foretold about her own life.

"If Sam can't make it outside, which of us can?" Amanda's voice wavered as she spoke, and Amy was shocked that she too felt the power that Sam's failure held over all the girls.

"I'm alone out there," said Emily, losing her happy persona for once.

"I've done drugs for so long. Sam was my role model. Transgendered, gay, addicted, a cutter? I figured I had it made in comparison, and if he could make it, it would be no biggie for me." Sophie was a girl Amy had little contact with, and yet her anguish spoke to the core of Amy's fear.

"Maybe it's just too hard," Amy ventured. "Maybe we're all just doomed to be screw-ups."

Everyone fell into a dejected silence as Mr. Adams sat, head down, slowly rubbing one palm against the other. Then in a very small yet compelling voice, he began, "Did you know that coal is dead, decayed plant matter that has been subjected to enormous forces of heat and pressure?"

What does that have to do with anything? But as if understanding her confusion, he continued, "Then, to make diamonds, that coal is burned up, crushed down and blown up out of a spewing volcano. Yet after that mountain vomits them out, there is nothing on this planet that is stronger, harder or more brilliant than a diamond."

Mr. Adams lifted his head up and let his eyes fall on each girl in the circle. "If regurgitated plant sludge can do that... just think what you can become."

Then, as if infused with some secret energy, Mr. Adams stood up, impassioned, animated and more forceful than the girls had ever seen him.

"Do not give up on yourselves. Do not. Yes, you are fragile. Yes, you'll get hurt. You'll get broken. But don't you see? That is the definition of 'human'. We are not gods. We are not infallible. We are human and we make mistakes. We *all* make mistakes."

He stood in the center of the circle, knees bent like a leopard ready to spring. But instead of springing forth to kill his prey, Mr. Adams was perched, ready to ignite his protégés. "But you and you and you... You are standing right on the very edge of your brilliance. We need you to pull yourself up and show us the shining light that lies within each of you. Don't give up on your quest. Take the next step and the next to claim your birthright and dazzle us with your radiance. This world needs your contributions. We all need your gifts. Have you been through it? Of course.

Do you have enormous obstacles to overcome? More than most. But that's how we get diamonds. That pressure and fire and violence is how we get the hardest, strongest, most enduring and beautiful substance on the planet. And, girls, *you* are life's diamonds."

Every girl sat frozen in that room, electrified by Mr. Adams' trust in them. Afraid to break the spell, no one moved. No one breathed.

Then out of the profound silence, Mia's quiet voice emerged with one simple word —

"Amen."

* * * *

Dear Diary,

So, it's official – I have no friends except Mallory.

I've written to everyone at home and no one writes back. Not even Stacey. Mom says she talked to them. I know she did. They're just not really my friends.

I thought it might just be because I'm not taking my meds. I'm starting to feel agitated and I'm getting mad easier, so I thought that might be making me mad at my friends. But that's not it. It's that I really don't have friends. I really don't.

It scares me because I realize that when I get out of here, I'll be totally alone. I have nobody except Mallory. Nobody.

Amy

Chapter Twenty-Nine

No matter how much she tried, Amy could not make the pieces go together.

Whoever invented puzzles is a sadist.

The girls were in the game room on Friday night. Amy had been rapidly gaining points on her way to the Create level of the Cs, and this was the reward for any girl making progress on their level. For Amy, it was a form of rebellion to cheek her meds with Mallory each morning, then go to class and comply with all the rules and lessons. Her deception felt like the ultimate triumph over a system that just didn't get what she was all about. So this reward felt like another act of pulling one over on the system, and Amy wanted to be sure that she participated.

Amy didn't like some of the more physical games because a few of the girls got really rough, but Jasmin had gotten caught gambling for toiletries, and as a consequence everybody lost the cards for a week. So now the choice was Scrabble or a puzzle. *Some choice.*

Mallory had zoned out on the sofa and refused to do anything. As Amy tried first one piece then another on the stupid puzzle, she became more and more agitated. "What the heck!" she finally said, throwing her puzzle piece across the table.

"B ticket, Amy." Ms. Pearl threw the punishment casually over her shoulder. "You know better than that."

Amy flounced over to the whiteboard by the door, wrote her name and 'B' next to it before stomping back across the room and flopping onto the sofa with Mallory.

"Don't!" Mallory snapped as Amy fell against her. "Leave

me alone."

"I just wanted—" Amy began, but Ms. Pearl stepped in immediately.

"Amy, scoot over and give Mallory some space. Can't you see she's in a bad mood?"

Before Amy could move, Emily was up and in her face. "You want to play Twister?" she asked as she grabbed Amy's hand.

"Do I look like I want to play Twister?" Amy growled, pulling her hand from Emily's.

Emily immediately dropped Amy's hand, looked hurt for a minute then skipped over to Mia to try again. Her eternal happiness just made Amy that much angrier. Twister was a dorky game. The puzzles were stupid. She wanted to play cards and was pissed that Jasmin had ruined it for everyone.

"Hey, Jas," she yelled across the room to the girl sprawled across the Twister circles. "I want to thank you for screwing up our card night. That was really considerate of you!"

"Amy! A ticket. Get another and you'll be removed from the room." Ms. Pearl's voice was sharp as she glared in Amy's direction.

"All right, all right," Amy mumbled as she headed toward the whiteboard.

"All right, all right, who?" Ms. Pearl usually didn't pull rank, but clearly she was addressing Amy.

"All right, all right, ma'am," replied Amy through gritted teeth. This night was clearly not progressing the way Amy had wanted and she really needed to leave and get some air. "Ms. Pearl, may I use the bathroom?" Amy asked, hoping for a reprieve from the forced camaraderie and joviality of the room.

"Yes, you may, Amy." Ms. Pearl turned to face Amy with her consent. "But use the time to get it together and settle yourself down. Understood?"

"Yes, ma'am," Amy replied as she ran from the room.

Amy took the long way around to the bathroom. She needed to walk. She wanted to run. She was so sick of the rules, the regiment and the self-righteousness of the staff. As she paced toward the bathroom, the *swoosh, swoosh, swoosh* of her slippers began to tap out a familiar backbeat to her heart. *Oh yes, yes*, she knew this feeling. *What was this?*

"Amy! What are you doing here?" Ms. Brooke's voice startled Amy and pulled her away from her thoughts.

"I'm going to the bathroom."

"Not this way you're not. That's a B ticket for being out of bounds." Ms. Brooke had started to turn when Ms. Pearl came around the corner.

"I was looking for you. Did I hear Ms. Brooke give you a ticket? That's three, Amy. Go hit the showers, you're done for tonight. Ms. Brooke, could you supervise?" Ms. Pearl asked as she headed back to the game room.

"Come on, Amy, get your stuff." Ms. Brooke walked Amy over to her room to get her things just as Mallory shuffled over to them both.

"I have to shower too," Mallory said to Ms. Brooke.

"Reason?" asked Ms. Brooke.

"I hit Emily."

"Why?"

"She fell on the sofa next to me and pissed me off." Mallory's voice was flat and her expression deadpan. Amy had seen Mallory like this before, but tonight she was too agitated herself to pay any attention.

"I hate this place. I hate my life," Amy began as they undressed outside their individual shower stalls. "You earn points, move up the Cs and *bam*! They hand out tickets, knock you down and make you go backward. There's no way to win at this stupid game. They have it rigged. They say they want you to Climb the Cs — find your way — create a new life. But they're all a bunch of liars. They just want to torture you. They just want us to fail and then stand around and say 'I told you so'. It's hopeless. There's no way to win and get the hell out of here."

Mallory was silently removing her shoes, socks and pants

while Amy ranted on, but she offered no encouragement and did not participate in the conversation.

"And it won't change when we leave. How many of your friends have written to you or called? Exactly none. That's how many. Same as me. As far as they're concerned, we're dead. Forgotten. Who's there for us? Your mom? I don't think so. She's probably happy to have all the booze to herself. My mom? 'Find your way, honey.' As if 'honey' makes her f-you any less hurtful. Why don't they just say 'good riddance', because that's what they mean...?"

Even as Amy stepped into the shower's spray, she could not stop herself from talking about the awful treatment she was being subjected to by everyone around her. Yet as the hot water splashed upon her head, there was a washing-away of some of her agitation. She scrubbed her head hard as she lathered her shampoo then remembered that she'd forgotten to give Mallory a palm-full of shampoo as she usually did. She thought about stepping out of her shower stall to offer but decided that Ms. Brooke might wonder why Mallory didn't have her own shampoo and get suspicious about what they were hiding in the bottle. *She can miss washing her hair one night*, Amy thought, and continued to vigorously scrub her own head.

By the time Amy finished her shower, her mood had settled and her anger abated. As she headed out of the shower, she noticed that Mallory had dropped her shampoo bottle on the floor of the shower. It was empty. Mallory must have poured all the dissolved pills down the drain while she showered, thought Amy. Maybe they'd start taking their meds again in the morning. Truth was, Amy was sort of wanting to take them again. She felt her agitation growing. There were nights her skin crawled with antsy-ness. She was beginning to realize how much better she felt with them. She'd talk to Mallory about it tomorrow. In the meantime, the hot water had soothed her enough that she longed for her bed. *Maybe I can actually sleep tonight.* Things would be better in the morning.

Chapter Thirty

Amy knew that Mallory was depressed, but it was beyond her how the girl could sleep through that God-awful buzzer in the morning. But there Amy stood, bed made, at attention by her bunk while Mallory stayed tucked in, still turned to the wall.

When Ms. Brooke came in to give the all clear, she scolded Mallory from the door, but when the girl still didn't move, she walked over to shake her. As soon as she did, Ms. Brooke turned to the roommates. "Girls, go get breakfast now. You can come back and dress later."

"Is Mallory all right?" they asked as if one voice.

"I said, go to breakfast." Her voice was calm and her face unchanged, but something in the tone made Amy's heart lurch.

"Is she—?" Amy began to ask, but before she could form a sentence, Ms. Brooke stopped her.

"I said go!"

Go. Go. Go. Go. The words began to tick off in Amy's head as she headed toward the kitchen. *Thump. Thump. Thump. Thump.* Amy's feet tapped out the rhythm of pain. *Ka-thunk, ka-thunk, ka-thunk, ka-thunk.* She could feel her heart beating in her temples, in her stomach, even in her palms. She could feel her mind going into that internal chasm when two staff ran past. From a distant place, Amy could feel the contagious panic in their voices. "OD'd," "gone," and "terminal," fell out as whispered clues were exchanged, only to explode once released and ricochet off the walls of the hallway as they ran. The taste of fear oozed across Amy's taste buds. Terror's bile built in the back of her throat. The pall of death hung in that room. The certainty of loss licked at her heels. There loomed the pit again, leering at her from the other side of this building manic. She could already feel it coursing through her veins as her vision began to close in on her and the black hole of the tunnel tried to suck her in. As she circled around in the vacuum of its grip, that black tunnel sucked out all hope. Hope for love. Hope for escape. Hope for a few moments of real, true happiness. A familiar tautness twisted her chest tighter and tighter.

As she entered the cafeteria, her last few moments of control lay at her fingertips. She ran to Ms. Avery for help — to tell her that a manic was coming — to ask to be removed to safety.

"Amy! Sit down!" came Ms. Avery's command as Amy lurched into the cafeteria.

"Help me!" she cried out. "I'm going to manic — "

"I don't believe you, Amy." Ms. Avery's anger was matched only by Amy's own panic. "You're such a drama queen. Knock it off and sit down. Isn't Mallory enough?"

Instantly Amy's consciousness retreated to the far corner of the room. Ms. Avery had said nothing — and yet, she'd confirmed everything. As her mind contracted in horror, Amy watched her body react like a wild animal to the overwhelming surge of emotions as she grabbed a cafeteria table and, with one blood-curdling roar, flung it halfway across the room at Ms. Avery. As it soared, the table knocked chairs, napkins and bowls in every direction. Mia and Emily, although safely to the side, ran from the room to avoid the mêlée.

Ms. Avery ran for the intercom as a wailing, pounding Amy continued to kick over tables and throw chairs, and within seconds three staff members came running into the cafeteria. As if watching another person, Amy saw them tackle her arms and legs and pin her to the ground while the screams and cries that came from the ground were wild and primal shrieks. In one coordinated move, the four staff members lifted Amy and carried her to Isolation, stripping her of all but her underwear before setting her carefully into the room and locking the door. There, inside the bared cement room, Amy's screams and shrieks reverberated off the walls for the next three hours.

Chapter Thirty-One

Only in strobe-light flashes was Amy aware of herself or her surroundings. She could hear her primal scream crash its rage against Isolation's cement wall before the sound floated up a half-octave then back down in a keening of unfathomable sorrow and grief. She felt the blunt force of that cool wall as her shoulder, dripping with sweat and snot and tears, smashed against it again and again and again in a satisfying bludgeoning against conscious thought. Her vision turned red, then white with rage in one moment when Ms. Prudy tried to confront her while in the next moment she fell sobbing into a fetal position on the floor.

Suddenly and without warning, Amy's anger took shape from the careening cascade of images that flooded her tortured mind. Red rage reared up like a beast ready to envelop her. Springing from the cement floor, its giant paw began to rise and slash as long, bloodstained claws loomed from the paw-pads. Its terrifying roar shook the walls and crumbled plaster from the ceiling while thrusting forward to pull her into its hold and the depths of insanity. Amy tried to roll away from the power of its lunge, but just barely escaped the carnage it hoped to elicit. "*Nooooo!*" she wailed. At the beast. At life. For Mallory.

They were lying. They just wanted to hurt her—show her.

Their lies became the fangs of the monster's teeth. Threatening, gaping, shining down at her as they swooped toward her throat—to kill her, to silence her, to stop the truth that was welling up through her hands to counter the beast's vileness.

"Mallory's not dead! Not, I say, not!" she screamed as she

threw herself again and again against the wall. In her rage, she began to rip at her panties, to twist them and pull them to use as some sort of weapon. What weapon, she knew not. She only knew she needed to use whatever she could to fight this foe attacking her or she would plunge into the dark hole of her madness never to again see the light of day. Swiftly, a staff member came in, quickly cut her panties off and fled behind the locked door. Amy's furious shrieks followed him out of the door. His dragon tail slithered out behind him as her screams became arrows attacking his green-scaled retreat.

Hour after hour, the demons of Amy's mind shrieked, screamed, kicked, beat and wailed out their rage and anguish. Hour after hour, she cycled down into the blessed abyss of insanity only to rise up into the unimaginable horror of reality and retreat into her terrifying tunnel again. With each cycle, the decision reared its head anew — should she stay in that blessed abyss and retreat from reality's pain, or should she claw her way back, feel the searing agony of truth and stay? With each cycle, the decision became more difficult, more confused, less sure.

Oh God, please, Amy began to pray. *Don't let Mallory be dead. I'll do anything —* anything *— to take it back.*

Amy stood up on wobbly legs and turned her face to the skylight at the top of her Isolation Room. Interlacing her trembling fingers, she raised them over her head and pointed them to the beam of light pouring in from the window overhead. "Please, God," she choked. "I beg of you…"

But there was no more. Her legs crumpled under her and Amy sank back to the floor until her face fell into the same tear-laden spot she had just abandoned.

Dead. Mallory was dead. And it was Amy's fault.

She had helped to provide the lethal cocktail Mallory drank in the shower. She'd helped to hide the fact that they were cheeking meds. She'd known the depth of Mallory's depression and had pretended that it didn't matter. She'd conspired with Mallory to get enough drugs to kill herself.

No. *She'd* killed her. Amy had killed her friend.

It didn't matter that she hadn't done it on purpose. It didn't matter that she hadn't intended to do it. It didn't even matter that she hadn't known what Mallory was going to do. She should have. She should have paid attention. *Oh God, I've killed my best friend.*

The keening sound erupted from deep in Amy's heart. A low, whale-song of a sound, it began to rise with the depths of her pain. Slowly, slowly the sound built as it rose in pitch and traveled up her windpipe like the trill of a Native American flute. The painful moan circled the room, glancing against each wall, the floor, and dancing along the ceiling before the haunting sound escaped out of the room in one hopeless cry. Amy lay, engulfed in the sound, naked, alone, curled as she had lain before she was born, and allowed the haunting song of sorrow to flood the room as it emptied Amy of all feeling, all hope, all love, with wave after wave of anguish.

Yet as the sound reverberated around the empty room, warmth began to engulf the girl. She rolled her head toward the light at the ceiling and let the sound fade from her throat. As she blinked at the light, Amy allowed the warmth to surround her nakedness. She became aware of her snot and saliva and tears and licked the sweet, salty taste of her sadness. Stillness crept into her heart and she lay, motionless on the floor, looking at the light.

As the minutes turned into hours, Amy sat in stillness. When she did, a new, unknown feeling began to enter the vacuum left by her sorrow.

As Amy's mind wrapped around the memory of her friend, she weighed her options moving forward. She could die, like Mallory. That was a thought.

She could rage for the rest of her life. Actually, that was what she had been doing.

Or she could be what Mallory had seen in her. But could she? Could she be amazing? Could she change the world?

In the light above her head, Amy saw the myriad diamonds of sparkling light that had clung to her shower door that day so long ago. But now, in this room, they were not the broken fragments of her rage. Now each one was the clean sparkle of hope. What if Mr. Adams was right? What if she was standing at the edge of her brilliance? What would it take to fall over that edge into the dazzling light? Could she? What if she failed?

There it was. What if she failed? As she focused on that light feeding into her soul, the question bounced at her again and again. What if she failed? Yet each time she asked the question, that pinpoint of light pulsed into her being, illuminating her soul and infusing her life.

Ms. Prudy had once scolded her to pull up her big girl panties and try. Was that the answer? And what if she tried and failed? What then? What if she gave it her all and it wasn't enough?

But this isn't working. I was always afraid to go all out because I wanted an excuse if I failed. But look at me now. Naked. Alone. Under surveillance in Isolation in an insane asylum. The tiniest smile began to curl the edge of Amy's lips. Clearly this wouldn't be anybody's definition of a successful coping strategy. *So now what*?

As she openly, earnestly asked the question, Amy felt another surge of energy and power enter the empty vessel that was her. What the—? What was this? What was happening? The strength of the surge made her sit up and caused her heart to jump in—what was she feeling?—fear maybe? Overwhelm? Her heart was pounding in her chest. In her throat. In her head. The surge grew and grew as that trickle of light became a beam then a floodlight. Her skin was radiant. Her hair iridescent. Light flashed out of her eyes. Beams shot from her fingertips. Amy took a breath deep into her lungs to counteract the energy and blew it out. Her breath shimmered out into the room with love, and clarity and strength.

Strength. This was strength. Pure. Unquestionable

strength. It surged through her being like illumination through a bulb — emblazoning every corner before spilling out vibrantly into the universe. The warmth of its light infused her with a feeling of power that she'd never known. With a sureness... Or? Or? Maybe...hope?

She sat up straighter, looking for someone to share this incredible feeling with — someone to help her continue her crawl from the depths... No, from these heights. Someone to share this moment that felt nothing short of...of...

As if summoned by Amy's thoughts, Ms. Prudy knocked on the window.

"Are you ready for me to come in, Amy?" she asked.

Amy nodded.

With a double click of the lock, Ms. Prudy stepped inside and the door was latched behind her. She held a light yellow yoga mat, which she handed to Amy to use as a blanket.

Through bloodshot, sunken eyes, Amy looked up from her curled position on the floor. "I have to tell you about what just happened..."

Chapter Thirty-Two

Amy was back on the dorm. After Isolation, they had lowered her status to Calming and placed her in an isolated unit to regain her bearings. While Ms. Prudy had tried to see Amy every day, Amy had refused and remained silent for days. The seclusion had suited Amy. With Mallory gone, there had been so much to consider. And Amy had needed time to sort out the battle she had waged in Isolation.

She knew if she told the medical community, they would say that she'd had a psychotic episode and dismiss her experience. But Amy knew better. Something had happened in that room and it meant something. Amy just needed to figure out what.

Silently, Amy had gone through the motions of Calming while deciding if she even wanted to live. Without Mallory, it seemed to be a rational question. Each breath had to be considered — willed into existence with a conscious effort to suck it in and blow it out. Each heartbeat had to be contemplated — would she allow them to continue or simply will them away? Each moment of sanity was a choice. Amy realized that the demons of her insanity could be summoned — she knew that falling into that abyss would, in some ways, be the easy way out of this pain. But she also realized that giving in to insanity would be a cop-out — maybe even, in her case, the coward's way out. But it was an escape. And too often it was an escape with the lure of the siren's song.

For otherwise there was reality.

"What makes you think you're responsible for Mallory's death?" Ms. Prudy's first question in therapy left no room for niceties or fakery, but instead cut straight to the chase.

"I murdered her."

"Did you?"

"And what would you call it?" Amy's voice quavered as she responded. "I knew she was depressed and yet I helped her stockpile pills…"

"Why?"

"Why what?"

"Why would you help her stockpile pills when you knew she was severely depressed?"

Amy pulled her feet onto the chair, folding her knees under her chin as she wrapped her arms around her legs. "Because it never occurred to me that she'd —"

"Stop right there," said Ms. Prudy as she lifted her palm to Amy's beginning torrent. "Did you hear yourself? It never occurred to you…"

Ms. Prudy waited a second for the sentence to sink in then continued her thoughts.

"You never intended to help your friend commit suicide. You certainly never intended to hurt her yourself. By definition, murder includes malice and forethought. You had neither. You simply did not murder your friend."

Ms. Prudy sat in silence until Amy's shoulders drooped and she leaned back into the easy chair.

"You did, however, break some very important rules — rules that, by the way, are set up to protect you girls against just this kind of tragedy. You are guilty of deception. You are guilty of not thinking things through. You are guilty of recklessness, thoughtlessness and conspiracy. And those acts led to a tragedy that you will have to live with for the rest of your life."

While Ms. Prudy's voice was soft, and infinitely kind, her words fell on Amy's heart like a sledgehammer. It was true. Life would never be the same. *She* would never be the same. Never. The weight of that knowledge lay on her heart like an anvil, pulling her down, sinking her soul into a darkness of sadness and wrenching loneliness.

"So what will you do?" Ms. Prudy's voice seemed to be coming from a million miles away as it pulled Amy back from the brink of her pain.

"What do you mean?" Amy blinked at the question. What the hell was she asking? *What does she want from me now?* Amy thought.

"This is your moment of truth, Amy. You have spent your young life making decisions as if there were no consequences. But some bells can't be un-rung. Is Mallory's death just another tragedy in your life of tragedy and sorrow — or do you find meaning in this moment and use it to build a future?"

"What future?" Amy whispered in a flat tone.

"So tell me about the warmth. You talked incessantly the night we released you from Isolation about the warmth. Tell me what happened in there."

Like a person awakening from a coma, Amy's senses began to clear and the vision returned in brilliant clarity. As the images CinemaScoped through her mind, her eyes widened at the recollection of the moment.

"It was amazing!" she began, dropping her feet back to the floor as she leaned in toward Ms. Prudy. "I've never felt anything like it. Someone — no, some*thing* — was there with me. I could feel the power of the presence…"

"And what do you think that was?"

"I don't know! I don't know! That's why I've been silent. I've been trying to figure it out. It just was. It was— I don't know. Big. And full. Overwhelming. Powerful."

"And why do you think it was there?"

"For me. *For me.* It was loving and caring. It was there for me."

"And what did it want to do for you?"

"Support me. Love me. Get me through this. It wanted to get me through this…"

"Why?"

"Why? I don't know why. I don't care why. It just did…"

"Okay, so what will you do with that knowledge?" Ms.

Prudy's question hung in the air. So many thoughts, so many feelings ping-ponged around in Amy's head, she could not sort them out. But it didn't matter. There was something…a warmth, a lightness, a…something that fed Amy's soul and surged into her heart. And in that moment, Amy decided that she wanted to live. And she wanted to live well.

Chapter Thirty-Three

Living well was easier said than done. No matter how hard she worked to really learn her academics, create a strong support system in her CD class and make honest progress in therapy, the truth was…she was completely and utterly alone. Sure, Emily was still in the bottom bunk. And Mia still shared the room. But for days after she returned, Mallory's bed lay undisturbed like some kind of cushiony monument to the stony-cold truth.

So when Ms. Pearl came to introduce the girls to Grace, who would be taking over Mallory's bunk, Amy had a cascading array of emotions. Chocolaty-skinned with an old-school Afro, Grace was, nevertheless, hostile and icy with her chin thrust out and her shoulders set. She barely acknowledged the other girls as she climbed up onto her bed, in G-A issued scrubs, and lay cross-armed and angry.

"Grace," Amy ventured quietly, "they'll ticket you if you sleep on top of your covers. Can I help you turn down your bed?"

Grace set her chin harder toward the ceiling over her bunk, blinked at the brightness of that ceiling overhead, but said nothing. Amy climbed up on her own bunk.

As she lay on her bed, Amy's mind went back to her own first day at Green Acres. She wondered if, under that angry façade, Grace wasn't as terrified as Amy had felt at realizing she was incarcerated. Her mind flipped from her terror at Myra's crazy outburst to her dismay at the reality of Climbing the Cs to her failure on the rock wall. But then other scenes began to intrude…like the amazing experiences in her CD class, the peacefulness she felt while hiking or her joy at pillow fighting with the girls. *Funny*, she thought, looking over at Grace's set face, *such little 'normal' things filled me with such happiness. I'd never have thought...*

And in the warm glow of those feelings, Amy fell asleep.

Like a boulder gathering speed as it rolls downhill, Amy began to climb back up through the Cs with more confidence and skill. She'd instantly sailed through Commit again, and with her excellent grades and equally superb participation in her chemical dependency class, she had conquered Conquer. Control had been trickier. With her new meds, Amy was very capable of controlling her angry outbursts but, of course, Green Acres required more than that. She also had to control her sadness and guilt and despair.

"I'm pretty sure you're the sickos here, trying to make me not feel sad for my friend," Amy had complained to Ms. Prudy after getting an A ticket for sulking. And while it was true that Amy had been exceptionally quiet since Mallory died, she didn't think her actions were inappropriate. After all, her best friend had died.

"Nobody's asking you not to feel—" Prudy began, but before she could finish Amy slowly lifted the A ticket up and pasted it across her mouth in reply.

"Okay, I know it feels like that, but here's the thing... You're alive. You have your whole life ahead of you. Clearly there's some bigger plan for that life—you felt it in Isolation. You know I'm right. Wearing ash cloth and moping around here will not inspire your life or encourage anyone else to follow your lead."

Amy pulled her knees up to her chin in her chair, but continued to look toward Ms. Prudy.

"Amy," Prudy continued. "You can play the tragic figure and live your life as a penance to your mistakes...or you can find the joy in small things, realize each day is a gift and use that gift to find some good—no, not 'find' some good—*create* some good in the world. It's time for you to step up from Control here and begin creating the world you want to live in. Is it always colored sad grays because you made some mistakes? Or do you take what you've learned from those mistakes and use that precious knowledge to paint the world your colors?"

"What if I have no colors to share?" Amy laid her forehead on her knees.

"That's a cop-out and you know it."

Amy had to look up at the harshness in Prudy's voice.

"What the —"

"Oh, please." Prudy was sitting forward now. "Cut the crap and just do it. If you want to walk around beating your chest and crying 'Mea culpa,' be my guest —"

"I don't even know what that means —" Amy's voice had edged into anger along with Prudy's.

"Of course you do. You sing it every day. It's become your theme song." Prudy made a fist and beat it against her heart as Amy had seen the saints do in old movies. Then, as she rocked back in forth to the beat of her fist, Prudy's voice rose in a singsong manner, "My fault, my fault, my fault, mea culpa, mea culpa, mea culpa..."

"Stop it!" whispered Amy, shaking with rage.

"You too," Prudy whispered back, staring straight into Amy's eyes. "You have a young, beautiful, potential-filled life — don't you dare throw it away playing some martyr. Mallory's dead. There's nothing you can do about that... except live Amy's life to the best of your ability. And you have tremendous ability."

The two of them sat staring into each other's face in a cold standoff. But then Amy's shoulders dropped.

"Cry yourself to sleep at night if you need to mourn your friend." Prudy's voice was soft and gentle now. "But get up in the morning, put on your best smile, and do good things in the world. Laugh. Play. Love, even. If you can't do those things for you, do them for Mallory. And then, one day, you'll do them for you. Don't let Mallory's death stay a tragedy. Let it change things — let it change you. In that way, she won't be forgotten."

* * * *

Dear Diary – Dear Mallory,

Prudy was such a bitch, she really got in my face. At first I was pissed at her, but then I decided to talk to you about it instead.

I miss you, Mal. I never had anyone I love die before. And I helped you do it. Why, Mal? Why'd you do it? I thought we were good. Wasn't I enough?

Prudy says I need to remember you by doing good things in the world. Happy things. But how the hell can I be happy when you're gone? And what the hell were you thinking to do that and leave me like this? I'm so pissed at you, Mallory. Then I feel guilty because I feel pissed. I'd like to see you just once so I could beat the crap out of you. No, no, I'd really just hug you. God, how can life be so messed up?

Mal, I'm going to try and do what Prudy says. If it's okay. I gotta get outta here and can't if I can't climb the Cs. But let me know if it pisses you off. I'll stop. I swear.

I miss you, girlfriend.

Love,

Amy

Chapter Thirty-Four

The salsa class had become a regular part of the PE program, but Amy still couldn't keep up with the dance steps. Ms. Prudy had given her an article off the Internet that talked about reprogramming the brain. It seemed scientists had found that certain body movements helped retrain pathways in the brain that had been lost to accidents or drugs. By reconnecting these pathways, it was possible to relearn things that had been lost.

It sounded like a bunch of mumbo-jumbo to Amy, but Ms. Prudy had promised that, if Amy tried it, she'd consider it Amy's Step-Up Activity into Create. Create, then Conclude, then freedom. It was all too enticing. Amy said yes.

So here she was, alone in the rec room during her few minutes of free time. She tuned to Habanero Hip-Hop and began to walk across the floor. As the beat kicked in, so did Amy's hips. She closed her eyes as the sound of the drums beat into her body and pushed her hips in a rapid swaying motion. She reached out and let her hands float to the sway of the guitar until, in her delighted blindness, they found the barre along the wall just as the synthesizer joined in and the beat kicked up. There, eyes closed, music pounding, Amy's inner vision focused on her feet. Back and forth, back and forth, she shifted her focus right and left as she picked up and put down each foot, lifting her heel and rolling to the ball of her foot before planting the other side and doing it again.

It took longer to stumble this time. Amy smiled. She'd been using the song's lyric to time her ability to dance without slipping. At first she'd only been able to dance for a measure or two at the most.

Amy's mind went back to the first time she had practiced alone. When her feet had betrayed her for the fiftieth time, she'd ended up a sweating, swearing mess on the floor. She'd sworn never to dance again and just forget it. Oh, how she'd wanted to give up and quit the whole project. But Prudy wouldn't hear of it and had sent her back. Anger had gotten her through the next rehearsal. Amy smiled. Anger had gotten her through a lot back then.

But now she was getting about two-thirds of the way through the song. She just stood at the barre, blocked out all competing vision except her inner desire, and let her feet find their way. And it was working.

Amy hit the button and started the song over again. She closed her eyes and grabbed onto the barre. Left-right, left-right, left-right, left-right... Amy felt the rhythm of her feet fall into place. Faster and faster the beat surged. Faster and faster her feet followed. Beads of perspiration began to form on her brow and, as her legs pumped and her feet listened to her commands, Amy delighted in the droplets of sweat dripping down her back and between her breasts. Her breath began to come in short pants and her heart's beat rose to match the beat of the music. Again and again and again her feet followed her commands until she passed the measure of the song where she'd failed last time. More...more...more... When her foot stumbled this time, she was nearly at the end of the song!

Amy let out a little yelp of triumph as she danced in a circle, pumping her arms into the air. In a few more days, she'd make it through the entire song. She just knew it.

Afterward, she did the exercises Ms. Prudy had given her to reconnect her brain. They had seemed really stupid when Prudy had first handed the picture guide to her. Kindergarten stuff, Amy had thought. But then she'd been shocked. The first exercise was simply to raise your right hand and your left leg. Amy had fallen on the floor! When marching while patting her thighs with her opposite hand,

Amy had had to concentrate with all her might to keep the beat and not trip. In the beginning, as soon as she stopped her intense focus, her hands instantly tapped on the same side. She wouldn't even notice for several beats at first.

But now she was getting good. Twenty exercises made up the routine. Each one was getting easier and easier. Her dancing was also getting better and better. So was her reading and her handwriting.

Prudy had told her it would happen, but Amy hadn't believed it. Now she had to admit that a lot of things were getting better. It was weird.

Amy looked up at the clock. Time to go. She had gotten permission to shower later so she could put in a good workout before bed. It made it harder to go to sleep at night — she would be excited about each day's accomplishments and it would be difficult not to think about them when she got to bed. But it was good.

CD class was getting even better too. Mr. Adams had asked her to consider chairing the class. There had been an open slot to chair since Sam had left. Amy had always coveted Sam's place as leader, but the position was filled by invitation only and, often, Mr. Adams just let it sit empty until he could find someone he believed was worthy of being an assistant.

Amy was deeply honored at the invitation.

In fact, Mr. Adams had given her the teacher's manual and marked out the first lesson he wanted her to teach. In addition, he'd given her supplemental materials that had fun activities to reinforce the lesson. He told Amy to choose an activity she wanted to do and prepare a visual for her part of the lesson.

Amy had decided that everyone would make mood masks. She'd found it really interesting when she looked at the long, long list of emotions in the teacher's manual. She realized that, when she first came to G-A, her list of emotions had consisted of pissed, really pissed and really, really pissed. She'd bet that's where Grace was living now, and had decided that knowing how to define other emotions might be helpful.

Amy hated to admit it, but she was finding joy in her life again. Occasionally this would make her feel guilty and she'd want to climb back into her pain, but then Mr. Adams or Prudy would remind her that Mallory would want her to live, and Amy would get it back together.

And, in fact, she had been doing so well that she was ready to Step Up to Create. She was going to put together the lesson plans for her CD class and perform a short dance for PE. Those were her Step-Up Activities. Then she would be just two steps away from home. She was thrilled.

* * * *

Dear Mom and Dad,

I did it! You should have seen my dance – it was the bomb. I had it all choreographed out, but I really worried about the chasse. I know, I know, I used to do them in my sleep, but it's been hard since – well, it's been hard. I can't keep the back foot following without tripping myself up. But I did it perfectly! And…get ready for it…I'M ON CREATE LEVEL!!!!!!!!!

You guys should really see me. I'm doing so good! Did you see my last report card? De bomb! And, Dad, did you see that B in geometry? Me? Who'da thought!

Oh, and now that I'm on Create, you get shrunk, too! It's Family Therapy time and we all get to start planning for me to be home! Yes! And I'll get to talk to you all every week now!

Did I tell you I'm mentoring this girl named Grace? Mr. Adams put me into the peer-counseling group. It's kinda fun. She's so angry. Reminds me of me. I've learned to listen and just say a few things to her. But I'm pretty good at it. I think it's easier when kids talk to kids because we know what it's like. No offense. But anywho, she's kinda tellin' me things. I can't tell you – only Ms. Prudy or Mr. Adams. But when she tells me about what it's like at her house, I'm glad you guys are my family.

I miss you. I love you.

Love, Amy

Chapter Thirty-Five

Amy loved that the higher levels offered so much more freedom, so when she forgot one of the supplemental books for her lesson planning in her CD class, she relished the privilege of walking back to her room to grab it.

As she turned the corner, she heard Emily's soft sobs as she lay huddled into a ball on her bed.

"Em," Amy began, softly rubbing Emily's shoulder. "What's up, girl? Why are you crying?"

"They don't want—" But Emily's sobs drowned out the rest of her sentence.

"Don't want what, Em?"

"Me!"

"Who doesn't want you?" Amy's heart knotted at the pure despair flowing from this strange little girl. For although she was sixteen, Emily was really about six in her heart.

"My mom—my dad—*everybody!*" Emily's cries had turned into shrieks.

"No, no, Em," Amy began. "That can't be. What makes you think that?"

"They *said* it!"

"No—"

"*Yes*, on the phone just now. They said it. And they already said it to Miriam, they said!"

Miriam was Emily's therapist, and if what Emily said was true, this wasn't good. Whatever Emily was getting to had already been approved by Miriam and was final. Amy's chest began to constrict in fear for Emily. She'd always thought Em's parents were hoity-toity bastards, but this was even worse than she'd thought. Even worse, and she didn't even know what it was.

"Tell me, Em…" Amy let the words hang in the air as Emily snuffled and coughed into her bed.

"Okay, okay, I'm not on Conclude, but I'm doing well. Right? Aren't I, Amy? Aren't I doing well?" Emily sat up and reached toward Amy.

"Yeah, you are, girl. You're doing well," Amy encouraged.

"I know. I am. So I asked to come home. Amy, I'm not like you or Kelly or Grace. I'm not mad. I'm not mean. No offense—"

"None taken."

"I don't get in trouble. Well, I do, but it's not 'cause I'm trying. I just forget things. Or get mixed up. I sometimes say things, but I don't mean to hurt people's feelings. I just sometimes don't read people well. Is that my fault?"

Despite the other girl's pain, Amy couldn't take it anymore. "Em, Em," she pleaded. "Just cut to the chase. What did they say?"

"Oh, oh, yeah. They said I can't come home until I'm eighteen no matter what. No matter what! *No matter what!*" And with that, she fell sobbing into Amy's lap.

As Emily snotted and sobbed all over Amy's legs, Amy stroked her hair and let her cry. How awful. What bastards. Just 'cause Em was odd didn't mean you warehoused her until she was grown. God, she felt sorry for the girl. Amy sat holding Emily as she cried and, despite herself, a single tear ran down her own face. Amy couldn't imagine the pain of being rejected by her folks like that.

Just then Ms. Pearl came in.

"What's going on here?" she asked as soon as she saw the girls.

"Em got some bad news from her folks," Amy offered.

The look on Ms. Pearl's face said she knew what the news was. Gently, she came over and picked Emily off the bed. "Come on, dear," she said, cradling Emily's shoulders in her arms as she led her out of the room.

"Thanks for your help, Amy." Ms. Pearl threw the

gratitude over her shoulder before guiding Emily in the direction of Miriam's office.

Amy sat on Emily's bed for a second to catch her breath then straightened Emily's blankets back to regulation, found her book and walked back to her CD class.

"But I like drugs and ain't nobody gonna tell me not to use."

Grace had begun sharing in CD sessions, but she was clearly not ready to move up to Commit. Grace's pursed lips were as locked in as was her denial. Slouched in her chair, the girl was totally enveloped in her anger and defiance.

"I liked them too," said Mia in a gentle tone. "They made me feel special when I felt all alone and like no one cared. Or, I thought they made me feel special. Then they didn't anymore. Then they started making me feel worthless, and skanky and more alone than I'd felt before."

Mia folded her hands in a prayer-like movement as she leaned in to Grace. "*Mi preciosa*, drugs are not your friend. They rob. They cheat. They destroy. They do not love. They do not help. They do not cherish."

"F-you!" Grace shot back, turning her back to Mia.

"Grace!" Mr. Adam's voice was sharp, but not unkind. "This is a safe place. We do not call names. We do not attack each other. That is a B ticket. I'll write it on the board for you. You," he said, walking to the board as he turned and pointed to Grace, "will take a breath, and try to express your feelings in a more appropriate manner."

Grace sat in silence. So did everyone else. What Grace didn't know was that the group was trained to stay silent until Grace attempted a redo. Amy smiled inside as she felt the power of the silence. She remembered when she'd been on the other side of this treatment and remembered the sheer torture of the seconds. Most of the new girls ended up in this position sooner or later. And usually gave in. It was just too hard to sit while everyone stared at you.

As the seconds ticked away, Amy was pleased as she watched the scene and realized how far she'd come since she'd sat in angry silence. Amy was sure that she had a handle on her drug use now. She'd thought she was doing better before Mallory's — before Mallory — but now she was really committed to getting her life together, and she realized how quickly drugs could get her off track. She was proud of how well she was doing in her dancing, proud of how she was doing in academics, proud that she was a peer counselor — even if her client was being obstinate right now — proud that she was to be the chair of the CD class.

"I don't care what you say, I can handle my drugs…" Grace's voice was quiet as she signaled surrender with her redo.

"I'm sure you think so, Grace." Mr. Adams responded to Grace's answer as if the conversation were just a continuing stream of thought. Amy glanced up at the clock — they'd sat in silence for three minutes. Amy marveled at his cool. When she chaired, she hoped to have his seamless way of pulling the girls along while keeping discipline so tightly wrapped. He was amazing.

"Class is over. Everyone — heads up — do the next five pages in your workbooks. Grace — do pages thirty-eight through forty-two and bring them to my office this evening. Okay, hang in, girls."

With that Mr. Adams turned to erase the board and Amy smiled. She knew what was on pages thirty-eight through forty-two. They'd kicked Amy's butt. She wondered how they'd affect Grace.

Chapter Thirty-Six

"Amy! Phone!"

Longer weekly phone calls were another privilege that came with Create and, as she hurried from her room to the phone bank, Amy was excited to hear her parents' voices.

"Hello?" she said as she took the phone from Ms. Avery's hand.

"Hi, honey!" As soon as her father's voice answered on the other end, Ms. Avery hit the timer button. Twenty minutes flashed on the digital face and instantly turned to nineteen minutes fifty-nine seconds. The clock was ticking.

"Hi, Daddy. How are you?"

"Oh, I'm good, sugar. It's good to hear your voice. How are things?"

"Really good, Daddy. Really good."

"I saw that B in geometry. Way to go, sport! Was it hard?"

"Yeah, especially finding slope. I just couldn't do that to save my life…"

"I know what you mean. Your mother still can't do it!"

Amy had to laugh at her father's playfulness, but as she did she heard another sound under her own voice.

"What?" Amy asked.

"It's me," said her mom. "I know I'm not good at math, but there are a lot of other things I can do."

"I know, Mom." Amy had to smile. Nothing had changed—even with so much time and distance between them.

"Just teasing, honey," laughed Dad.

"Yeah, yeah," said Mom, but teasing was in her own voice.

"We have something to tell you," said Mom, clearly changing the subject.

"What?"

"You've been approved for a home visit!" Mom's and Dad's voices blended in an imperfect chorus as they tried to both tell her the news at the same time.

"What? When? For how long?" Amy barely got the words out before her throat closed and tears sprang to her eyes.

"Next week. Overnight. Tuesday until Wednesday. Oh, honey, we're so glad you're coming. We miss you so much!"

Amy couldn't answer. She was crying too hard to speak.

"It's okay, baby. We'll be together soon. Do you want something special for dinner?" There was Mom, always going for the practical. But it worked. Amy was able to harness her tears as she considered all her mom's best recipes.

"Spaghetti."

"Okay," said Mom.

"Look, honey," Dad began. "I have to get back to work, but I'll see you on Tuesday. I miss you, Amy. Talk to your mom."

"Bye, Dad."

"Bye, baby."

"Mom?"

"I'm still here."

"Mom, does anybody ask about me?" Amy didn't know why that came out. She hadn't thought about her old friends that much since... Since that day. But now it seemed of utmost importance. Yet her mother's long silence made Amy's heart sink.

"How about you just plan on spending time with us, honey?" Her mom's evasion answered the question.

"It's okay, Mom. I'm just so glad to be coming home."

"Me too, sweetie. Me too."

Just then the timer rang and Ms. Avery appeared.

"Gotta go, Mom. Bye."

"Bye, baby. I love you."

"Love you too."

As usual, Ms. Avery let Amy listen to the click of her mother's phone line before she took the receiver. And, as usual, Amy cried her way to class.

* * * *

Dear Diary – Mallory,

I wasn't going to tell you this because I was afraid you'd be disappointed in me. But then I knew I had to tell you the truth.

I got my first home visit on Tuesday. It was so weird. Everything looked like I was in one of those circus fun houses. It all looked the same. But different. Like I was looking at it through one of those crazy mirrors. Just a little jiggly and a little off kilter. But it was good. I loved seeing Mom and Dad again – I even liked Lizzie. Ain't that a hoot! We ate Mom's spaghetti and Dad made his famous chocolate cake – it's the only thing he can make! And everybody told stories and laughed around the table. Then we watched movies and went to bed.

Well, THEY went to bed.

I went out.

I don't know what I was thinking, but I just needed to see everyone. God, I feel awful about the whole thing, but here goes.

Dad left his cell phone out, so I called Stacey and Kairyn. What did they expect – they're my best friends? Anyway, I went out the back door after Mom and Dad were asleep and met the girls at the park.

It was great to see them. They told me about what was happening at school and – did you know? – Andie's pregnant. She's sixteen! Sucks for her. Anyway, anyway...oh well, here goes. Stacey brought X. Can you believe it? She started teasing me about being a goodie-two-shoes from my new little school and pressed it into my hand. I was shocked. I told her I'd been sober for ten months... and she just laughed! "Goodie girl, goodie girl, goodie, goodie, goodie girl!" she sang as she bumped her hip into me.

Mal, I looked at it for the longest time. Do you have any idea how much I really still wanted it? It was pink. I know the color doesn't really make any difference, but I liked the pink ones best. Don't know why. Just did. Stupid, huh?

But I didn't take it.

I didn't.

And when I didn't, Stacey got pissed. Said I thought I was better than her. And she grabbed Kairyn and stomped off. And Kairyn went. She doesn't even do X. She used to bug me when I did. And she went. The bitch.

I had to walk home by myself. God, I was pissed. They were supposed to be my friends and look what they did? Give me X. Leave my ass. That's friends? Don't think so.

So, that's it. I don't have any friends to come home to. I realize that's why I went out. I needed to know. But, Mallory, I never expected that answer. I just thought they'd always be there for me. Crap.

And to make matters worse, you know who I saw on my way home? Yeah, you know. The night sucked. So what's the suckiest thing you can think of? That's right. J-J with Kiera. Skank of the week. He saw me too. Freakin' walking alone in the middle of the night. I saw him pull her even closer to him — like there was any room — and smirk at me over her head. Bastard. How could I ever think that I liked him? What a jerk.

And because I snuck out, I can't tell anyone. The whole thing sucks. And now I have nobody. You freakin' killed yourself, Mallory. And you left me alone with these lowlifes and losers. How could you? How could you?

Amy

Chapter Thirty-Seven

"I'm sorry I couldn't get to you earlier, Amy," Ms. Prudy began. "I usually try to see students as soon as they get back from home visit, but we had an emergency here. But Mr. Adams tells me that something's going on with you. You want to tell me about it?"

"No."

"Okay, Amy. That doesn't get us very far. Why the regression?"

"I don't want to talk."

"If this is your response to a home visit, maybe you're not as far along the Cs as we thought you were..."

"I can't tell. I'll lose my bed. I'll lose my status. I can't go all the way back!"

"Whoa, whoa!" Ms. Prudy put her hand up like a traffic cop. "Who told you that? Why in the world would we punish you for telling us the truth? That's a little draconian, don't you think?"

"But Kelly said..." Amy began.

"Kelly? That's your authority? How reliable is that source?" Then, as Amy looked at Prudy, Prudy began to smile. "Think about it."

"Okay, maybe you're right. But I screwed up."

"Most girls do."

"No, really..."

"So tell me about it."

"I snuck out and almost took X." As soon as the sentence escaped, Amy's shoulders dropped. It felt like she'd been holding the weight of that secret forever. Whatever the punishment, it was good to have that oppressive silence gone.

"'Almost' being the operative word here," said Ms. Prudy without hesitation. "Tell me more."

Without taking a breath, Amy poured out the story of Stacey, Kairyn and J-J. She vomited her loss and betrayal and pain. She threw away her sadness and self-doubt and loneliness. And, after the whole story was told, she was wrung out and empty.

"Wow." Ms. Prudy sat back in her chair as if the tide of Amy's words had washed her away too. "It sounds like a lot of good things happened there."

Amy was dumbfounded.

"Good? Are you nuts? I lost everything. I nearly rolled! I lied to my folks! Can you spell 'screw-up'?"

"Amy, that's not how I see it," countered Prudy. "I see a girl who has faced some cold, hard realities in her life. I see a girl who withstood temptation and said no. I see a girl who feels guilty about lying. I see someone who is ready to deal with reality head-on. Can you spell 'amazing'?"

As Prudy spoke, Amy looked at her face hopefully. But after a moment, that hope fell away and dejection took over.

"Maybe," Amy began. "It's true, I didn't take it. But I wanted to. And what's so good about realizing you have no friends? I'm not sure it's not better to live a fantasy than know you're all alone."

"As far as the X is concerned, you'll always want to. That's addiction. I know people who haven't used for thirty years and still wake up wanting to. That's just the nature of the beast. But you didn't. And that's huge." Ms. Prudy raised her eyebrow at Amy to accentuate her point.

"And as far as friends go—you can't start fixing it if you don't know what the problem is. You've changed. Your old friends haven't. They may never. But it doesn't matter. You can't go back. The good news is—now you know. You know they're not there for you. But they never were. You just fantasized that they were. You're past that fantasy now and can start building on reality."

Amy looked up at Prudy and just rolled her eyes.

"No, this is good. You're now free to really start building your new life. You're free to leave that old skin behind and wiggle out in the new, improved version of you. Spread your wings and fly away, girl."

"Maybe."

"No maybe—really. You've taken the first steps by facing reality and facing your addiction. Now you're ready for the next step—"

"What?" asked Amy.

Just then, Ms. Prudy picked up the phone and began to dial. "Telling your parents that you snuck out and lied. It's time to build on your integrity."

"No!" cried Amy as she realized just whose number Prudy was dialing.

"Hi, Mrs. Miles? Prudy at Green Acres here. Good, and you? Oh, I'm glad. Amy's here to talk to you, do you have a minute? Okay, here—" And with that, she handed Amy the phone.

"Hi, Mom." Amy could feel her voice quavering as she spoke.

"Hi, honey. What's up?"

"I have something to tell you."

"Okay, what?"

"I snuck out of the house when I was home and I didn't tell you."

"I know."

"You do?"

"Uh-huh."

"Oh no. Why didn't you tell me?"

"I was waiting for you to tell me."

"Oh, Mom, I'm so sorry."

"I know." Her mom paused a moment, then asked, "So, why did you leave?"

"I thought I had friends to see."

"And did you?"

"No."

"Oh, I'm so sorry, honey."

"Me too."

"So what are you going to do next time?"

"I will ask, Mom. Really. It all sucked and I couldn't tell you how sad I was because I'd lied and then I just had to feel crappy all by myself—"

"Amy, it's going to be hard when you come back. You have to build a whole new life for yourself. And you have to do it alone—"

"I know, Mom. I know."

As she spoke, Amy looked up and saw Ms. Prudy's hand reaching for the phone.

"Well, I gotta go, Mom. I love you."

"'Love you too, honey."

"Hi, Mrs. Miles," said Prudy. "Let's continue this conversation on Family Therapy Day, if that's okay."

"That would be great."

"Thanks, Mrs. Miles. We'll talk to you later."

"Goodbye now."

"So," said Prudy, hanging up the receiver and turning toward Amy, "do you feel better now?"

"Yes, I do."

"'Thought you would."

"So do I lose my bed?"

"Absolutely not. You just took responsibility for your actions. Honey, you've been under tight regulation for months now. It's not unusual for you to go a little wild with freedom on your first time out. But what you really need to learn is self-regulation—not G-A Way regulation. You messed up. But you fixed it. That's an important learning opportunity. Why in the world would I punish you for that? Now if you'd lied to me here? Well, that's a different story. So don't lie!" Prudy playfully pushed at Amy's leg and, in so doing, seemed to release all the fear and tension that Amy had been holding on to regarding her home visit.

That night, as she crawled into her bed, Amy was actually happy to be in the safety and custody of Green Acres. She fell asleep, not confined, but cocooned, and safe and free.

* * * *

Dear Diary – Mallory,

We all talked about my sneaking out during Family Therapy. The truth is, it felt good to just say it and not have to lie. We all made rules and consequences for my running away, and get this, rewards for behaving. My allowance will now be tied to my good deeds. Little Susie Scout, I guess.

There's part of me that really wants to go home. I miss my home. I miss my folks. I miss my sister. I miss my life.

But there's part of me that is terrified to go. I know I'm safe here and I know what to expect. What's that saying? The devil you know. Yeah. I'd rather be here with the devil I know than have to go out there all alone into…what?… What does lie ahead for me? What?

Mallory, if you're up there, let me know what's out there. I'm scared.

I love you and miss you,
Amy

Chapter Thirty-Eight

Emily had settled right in again after her painful phone call. Amy was sure that, in truth, Green Acres was more of a home for her than her parents' place had ever been. It wasn't long before the girl was her bouncy, annoying self.

As she'd reconciled herself to the long stay, Emily and Mia had become fast friends. To see the gawky pigtailed Aspie with the tiny dark beauty was amusing. Amy thought they looked like a couple that might be drawn for a cartoon series when they stood together. But neither seemed to mind. Emily let Mia fix her bright red hair and do her makeup and Mia seemed content to play big sister to her much taller friend.

Amy's chairmanship of the CD class was going well. Both Mr. Adams and the girls had commented regularly about what a good leader Amy was. Mr. Adams had talked to Amy about forming her own CD teen group once she graduated from Green Acres. They had even talked about Amy becoming a drug counselor as a career choice. She'd really thought about it as she seemed to have all the right skills for it.

Or maybe not.

Amy knew she was a good teacher and leader for most of the girls, but she really couldn't handle Grace. And now, as Amy sat in the cubicle she occupied while providing peer counseling, she saw Grace heading in her direction.

Oh crap, thought Amy, *fifteen minutes left and I could have been out of here free and clear. Instead, here comes Bitch-Bitch-Snarl.* In fact, Grace's constant complaining and hostile mood had earned her the nickname from nearly every girl on the dorm. The girl was permanently stuck on pissed and seemed incapable of discovering any other mood, and now she was Amy's responsibility until the end of her shift.

"'Yo, bitch," Grace snapped as she slumped into the chair opposite Amy.

"Hi, Grace, what's up?" Amy tried to put her best professional counselor face on but was sure Grace could read her dislike.

"I'm here," Grace said, tightening the fist she was drumming on the table until her knuckles turned a rich cream color.

"So you are…"

Nothing.

Amy lifted her eyebrow toward a silent Grace. Still nothing. She shrugged and opened her hands to elicit a response. But Grace gave nothing back.

"Grace, do you want to talk, or do you want to just waste my time?" *Damn!* Amy thought as soon as the words escaped her mouth. *That's not what I wanted to say. How unprofessional can I get? And yet, this girl just makes me cringe.*

At that moment, Amy had all she could do to suppress a smile. Grace was so much like Amy had been when she first came to Green Acres, and the irony of the situation was not lost on her. How often had Ms. Prudy or Mr. Adams sat in front of her while she pulled this same taciturn crap on them? *Okay*, she thought, *I guess I can sit here and stare at her sour face. I sort of deserve it.*

Suddenly Grace exploded into language. "So, they made me come see you — all right? I'll lose my bed if I don't start participating in counseling and you'd be it. Get it? I don't wanna be here but I hate sleepin' in Isolation. Okay? This place sucks. You suck. This whole thing's stupid. And so are you, you pantywaist little bitch."

"Okay," replied Amy, proud of her ability to hear what Grace was saying and not let it push her buttons. "You're clearly unhappy here. It's good you can say that. So what are you going to do about it?"

"Don't give me that crap! Ya know I can't do anything!" Grace crossed her arms across her chest and turned her back in Amy's direction.

"Of course you can. Here's the deal, Grace — what you're doing isn't accomplishing anything. You can keep doing the same things, but how's that working for you? Or you can try something new. Look, they've got the key. Literally. They aren't gonna let you out until you climb the Cs. You can piss and moan and kick and scream and just stay here forever, or you can get with the program and get the hell out of here. But, girl, there just isn't a third way."

"I should become a little kiss-ass like you?" Grace fairly spat the words at Amy.

"Well, this little kiss-ass is one step from home and you're about to lose your bed. You tell me what's working and what's not."

"Fuck you!"

"I won't report that."

"Report it! I don't give a fuck —"

"Oh please. It's not like we can't all say it — and do. It's just the rest of us are smart enough not to do crap like that that makes us lose our beds. You can be stupid or smart here. Fight the system if you want to. But look around. Green Acres doesn't care if you stay until you age out — it's just more insurance money for them. The only one who loses here is you."

Grace's face stayed its same hard stone, but as Amy spoke, she stopped glaring and looked Amy's way.

"Grace, I was like you when I came. I hated this place. Still do. But then I realized that there is only one way out and if I ever wanted to leave here, I had to play by the rules. But truthfully, was your old life working? Mine sure wasn't. I'm going to try it their way for a while because if I'd kept up the old way, I'd be dead."

Amy hadn't even finished her last word when Grace stood up and walked out of the cubicle. Amy wasn't sure if she'd gotten to her or just pissed her off. But the whole scene made her question if she wanted to spend the rest of her life working with such angry, screwed-up people.

Later, as she relayed the session to Mr. Adams, she had to ask him, "How do you do it?"

"Me?" he began. "I love the challenge. I pay strict attention to the closed down, angry faces that first walk in this door. The reward for me is that first time you see their softness break through. The gift is that shining that lies just behind their eyes. That brilliance of their inner being that, so often, I get the privilege of watching emerge. Amy, I wouldn't change careers for a million dollars. Watching all you girls come into your own makes me one of the richest men on the planet."

"Yeah, I can tell," grinned Amy. "That beat-up old Civic out front really proves your wealth."

Mr. Adams smiled back and Amy was sure that, like her, he was remembering how shut down and angry she had been not too many months ago.

"So what do I do about Grace?" she asked, getting back to the problem at hand.

"Stay with her."

"For how long?"

"As long as it takes."

"But how will I know how to help her?"

"You just will. Trust your instincts. She'll let you know what she needs. And you'll know what to give."

"I hope you're right, but I doubt it."

"Trust me." Mr. Adams smiled and winked at Amy. Reassuring as he meant to be, Amy wasn't sure she'd ever get to Grace. *Maybe some cases are just hopeless*, she thought as she left his room.

Chapter Thirty-Nine

Okay, she could smile. But, that didn't change the fact that some total sadist had designed the Step-Up ceremonies at Green Acres. This was it. Her last Step Up. She was moving on to Conclude and her next Step Up would be graduation from the program. So, the rules said that she had to go back and repeat her 'worst' Step Up and correct her failure. What idiot had thought of that? If she failed the first time, what made anyone think she would succeed the next?

And yet, there was just the tiniest part of her that was excited. No, no, make no mistake about it—there was a much bigger part that was totally terrified. But what if? What *if*?

Looming in front of her was the same twenty-four-foot rock wall that had defeated her the last time. Its rough-hewn face, protruding edges and treacherous crevices seemed to smirk down at her, daring her to scale their heights. The salmon-colored spotlights seemed to accentuate the steep face and hidden handholds.

"Amy, up!" Ms. Avery seemed to relish ordering Amy to the wall. Carefully, looking only out of the corners of her eyes, Amy was sure she saw Avery's lips curve up in triumph over Amy's clear nervousness. But Amy quickly pulled her eyes away, concentrated on breathing and focused on the wall. *Not today*, she thought. *You will not beat me today*. And breathing that mantra in and out, Amy stepped up to the wall.

"Go, giiirlll. Go, giirlll. Go! Go!" Emily and Mia had thrown their arms around each other and were chanting while they step-kicked like Rockettes. Amy didn't have to turn around to realize the silliness of the unlikely pair as they burst into peals of laughter and nearly fell on the floor.

But Amy's focus was straight ahead.

The familiar warmth of the rock surface was the first thing Amy noticed. All those hands grabbing it, rubbing it, brushing it had warmed the surface in a surprisingly friendly way. As Amy's foot found one outcrop and another, she began to gasp and blow hard and the sandpaper surface of the rock began to make her fingertips hot with friction. As she ascended, Amy kept looking up and down for hand- and footholds along the way. When she did, her helmet would bump against the wall, making an echoing beat against the inside of it. Startled by the sound at first, she soon listened for its reassurance that she was, in fact, making steady progress.

A giddy high began to envelope her. Amy was breathing hard and loud, the rhythm of that breath was punctuated by the suspension of her foot in the air followed by the deep satisfaction of the thud and scrape as it planted itself on the next outcrop…and the next…and the next. Every muscle in her body was hot with tension and release, every nerve was sending signals of danger and escape. Adrenaline coursed through her veins, making her vision more crisp while amplifying her hearing.

The higher Amy climbed, the more the high boosted her. *Things are going too well*, she thought. *This seems too easy.* She realized that her only fear was that she was afraid of not being afraid. And that realization made her stop mid-climb. With one hand stretched high above her head, her ear pressed against the side of the wall under her small bike helmet and her beet-red face pressed against the wall's relatively cool stoniness, Amy froze. She took one breath then another of the wall's strong mineral smell as she paused her thoughts.

"Go, giiirlll. Go, giirlll. Go! Go!" Mia and Emily began their chant again. The sound echoed off the top of the wall, bounced around the room and landed on Amy's exposed back.

"Amy? Come on, girl! Don't stop now!" Ms. Avery's voice sounded far away as Amy looked past her hands and saw how high up on the wall she'd climbed.

"Amy? Amy?" Ms. Avery's voice now barely registered as the lights and shadows of the room filled Amy with warmth.

With slow determination, Amy began to push herself up to the next foothold. She heard her shoe scrape against the rough stoniness of the wall. She felt the coolness of the rock against her fingertips as they clung to the next handhold and the next and the next in this new, uncharted space where no previous hands had imparted their warmth to the stone. Inside her, her heartbeat began to change. Coupled with the pounding exhilaration of her physical activity, Amy could feel the increasing beat of excitement as the top of the wall loomed closer and closer. *I'm going to do it*! The thought burst into her head before her mind even realized it was a possibility. *Oh God! Look! Look*! Amy had to blink hard to actually watch her hand touch the flag at the top of the wall. Her whoop was involuntary as that same warmth that had invaded, caressed and expanded her inner being in Isolation returned to fill her, support her, and…yes… empower her to the point of bursting.

I've done it! I've really done it! Amy wrapped her fingers around the red silkiness of that flag and thrust it up over her head.

Down below, the girls all began to scream, clap and jump around. Amy turned to look down at all the commotion — and…she looked. With no fear, no vertigo, no anxiety…she allowed her eyes — her spirit — to take in every detail. And, at that moment, she knew that Mallory was watching too.

No longer able to control the explosion of emotions erupting inside her, an elated cry escaped Amy's lips as she issued her thumbs-up to be lowered down.

As soon as she touched down, the girls all crowded around Amy, laughing and cheering. But although Amy's feet had touched the ground, her spirit was still there at the top of that wall.

* * * *

Dear Diary,
I got a home visit! It was great!
No screw-ups. None.

Mom and Dad have painted my room to get ready for my homecoming. It's all getting pretty exciting. But sad and scary at the same time. I know now that I don't have any friends. I was home for three days and not one friend called me. I was so bummed. Not one.

But we signed me up for dance classes, and NA meetings, and enrolled me in a new school. I'll also be joining the youth group at church and they're going to build a shelter for homeless moms and their kids. So, anyway, I guess I'll be busy.

I think that's the key. I gotta stay too busy to go hang out with those other guys. But it doesn't matter. I talked to a few people I know on Facebook and can't believe I ever wanted to be friends with them. Their walls are all about chugging, or rolling, or sexting. That's just not me anymore. Funny, I didn't even know it until I messaged them.

Oh, did you notice that I'm not writing to Mallory? Don't need to. Something happened at the top of that wall. I saw her. I felt her. I felt her loving me. And we said goodbye. I'll always love her, but I don't need to feel bad about her anymore. Whatever she gave me up there is in here. And that's good.

Love,
Amy

P.S. ONE MORE WEEK! They just told me I made it! I'm graduating and I'm so excited. Mom and Dad are coming to pick me up and then I go home. Home. Can you believe it? I can't wait. ONE MORE WEEK! ONE MORE WEEK! ONE MORE WEEK!

* * * *

Surprisingly, nostalgia lingered around every corner. Amy had never thought that she would actually ever miss Green Acres Academy. But now that graduation hovered over her shoulder, everything took on a sentimental twist. The last time she'd have Taco Tuesday. The last time she'd dance to the Hot Salsa DVD. The last time she'd hike the forest trail. The last time they'd do Girls' Night In.

But this might be the biggest. It was the last night that she would chair the CD class. Of everything that she had done at Green Acres, Amy was proudest of her work as a leader of the chemical dependency group. When Sophia and Tasha had first come to the school, Amy had been instrumental in turning them around and getting them onboard with the program. Now Tasha was coming along and had become best friends with Grace. Tasha was even moving up the Cs at record speed. Amy had successfully counseled Andrea when she returned high from a home visit and helped Niki realize that she really, really had to kick her speed habit. As Amy looked around the room, face after face brought back memories of successes and turning points. She was actually pretty proud of herself.

"I know it's tempting out there," she began when it was her turn to lead the meeting. "I won't tell you that I won't make mistakes—I've already done that once on a home visit. I also won't tell you that I'm not scared—I'm terrified. I know how easy it might be to toss my discipline and plunge into insanity and addiction. But I will tell you that I have a whole arsenal of tools to help me make other choices. And my intention is to use them."

Several girls began to applaud at Amy's declaration.

"We've all been through a lot here. Life is harder for us as is. But I think what we've all learned is that drugs don't make it easier—just harder and more complicated. I'm committed to finding straight friends, to staying straightedge, to attending meetings. I know I can't do this alone. I'll need meds and therapy and, maybe, an understanding boss… and maybe regular 'vacations' to a place like this. That's the way it is. I'm hoping not to trip. But if I do, I'm determined to stand up, brush myself off and try again."

A few girls murmured "Yeah" and "You go, girl" as she spoke, and listening, Amy found more of her voice.

"Take advantage of this place. I know some of you hate it. I did. But it helped me find my essence and my voice. It helped me find things in me that I didn't know existed. Find those things in you. And use them to make a good life for yourselves."

Amy shifted in her chair as she grabbed Mia's hand. Mia grabbed Emily's, who grabbed Tasha's and soon all the girls were joined in a circle.

"Okay, so we're mentally ill. They say a little madness is necessary in every genius. Let's just say we're all on our way to finding our genius — and then, let's go find it!"

Amy lifted her clasped hands and the rest of the girls followed suit before breaking into excited applause. For all the girls who stayed behind, Amy knew her current success would be a lifeline as they struggled to find balance and health. So as the meeting ended, there was no lack of hugs and air kisses as the girls found closure in Amy's pending departure and simultaneously planned for the coming graduation, or Climbing the Cs, party.

Mr. Adams was surrounded by girls asking questions and jockeying for his attention as they discussed decorations or the order of the program. But as the planning and back patting continued, Amy caught sight of Grace slipping out of the door and heading down a restricted hallway. *What's this?* Amy thought. Something in Grace's behavior set off red flags in her brain and tightened Amy's chest.

While the other girls continued to chat and reminisce, Amy slipped out of the door and followed Grace down the forbidden hallway. Off behind housekeeping and food services, the corridor had numerous doors, cream-painted walls and a solid linoleum floor. Bare and utilitarian, the corridor led to nowhere. There was no reason for Grace to choose this place.

Just as the laughter and chatter began to fade behind her, Amy heard the crash of glass ahead of her and quickened her step.

There stood Grace, covered in blood, a shard of glass cutting into her hand.

"Grace, stop!" Amy ran up to the other girl, coming within two feet of her. Grace had smashed her fist through the fire extinguisher glass, grabbed a shard and slashed her left wrist. Blood covered her torn knuckles and the clean, open line of her wrist. More red oozed from her hand as she gripped the shard with such force that the blade was clearly cutting into her palm. Her face was soaked with rivulets of tears and her painful expression seemed to be more the result of anguish than the sting of her gaping wounds.

At Amy's command, Grace lifted her hopeless eyes. She held the blade up high and turned the point toward the vein in her neck.

"Get back!" she screamed as Amy approached.

"Okay, okay," Amy agreed, holding up her hands in a surrender motion. "Grace, don't do this. Don't do this, girl."

"Why not? Huh? Gimme one good reason…"

"Because your life is worth something—"

"Yeah, right. Tell that to my mom who tossed me away here—"

"Hey, girl. We've all been tossed. But I don't think it's away. I think it's for a second chance—"

"Bullshit!" Grace gesticulated toward Amy with her blade and droplets of blood splattered like spring rain.

"I thought bullshit too when I first came here. I didn't think I wanted to be saved and have to live in the world. I didn't think I was worth saving. But I was wrong. And so are you…"

"What do you know?"

"I know that Tasha loves you. I know that I loved Mallory. She nearly killed me too when she killed herself. I know that I'll never live another day of my life that I won't wonder why Mallory chose to leave me rather than accept my love.

I know that if you do this thing you will hurt Tasha for the rest of her life..."

Grace's shoulders fell just a little and she looked down at the pool of blood forming on the ground by her feet. "I just can't — " Her tears now turned to sobs as her eyes pleaded with Amy.

Amy held the other girl's gaze by a thread. She knew that this was the moment of truth. Time slowed to a crawl, allowing Amy to study this girl. Could she pull her in with that fragile thread she held? Amy's mind raced back to her own desperate, destructive behavior. She knew the hell Grace was skirting. She knew the deep longing to fall back, dive in and escape to oblivion. And yet, there was something in Grace's eyes...some desire for rescue. She knew how that felt and she reached for it in this girl.

"Grace, I also know that this pain will go away. Maybe not today, but someday. And probably someday soon. It's temporary. But death is forever. And loss is forever. If you can't bear it for yourself — bear it for Tasha... Grace? Grace?"

With a keening sob, Grace began to crumple to the floor as her shard of glass clinked and clattered onto the linoleum. Amy ran up and grabbed her before she could hit the ground, but the weight of her limp body pulled both girls to the floor. Amy squeezed her hand over Grace's wrist and gripped hard as blood squished out from between her fingers and dripped down onto her legs.

"Help! Help!" she cried into the air.

Emily was the first to hear and came hurrying down the corridor. Upon seeing all the blood, she froze, slapped her hands over her mouth and clamped her eyes shut.

"Emily! Get help! Hurry!" Amy cried as Emily shook her head emphatically no.

"I can't!" she mumbled behind her clasped fingers as her feet remained rooted to the spot.

"Emily, look at me! Just me! Good girl — look at my face." Despite her pounding heart, Amy had lowered her voice and let her words emerge ever so slowly as she cradled the bleeding Grace in her arms. The strength of Amy's will alone forced Emily to open her eyes and gaze at Amy.

"Go — get — help — now," Amy commanded. As if released from a spell, Emily dropped her hands and ran.

All the while, Amy held Grace, shushing her, cooing to her, stroking her blood-soaked hair and sweat-drenched face as she comforted the girl and held pressure to her wrist.

Within seconds, Mr. Adams arrived. In a seamless movement he pulled a handkerchief from his pocket and pressed it against Grace's wrist as his other hand hit the button on his walkie-talkie. "Code blue! Hallway fourteen!"

Instantaneously, staff came running from every direction. Girls were ordered back to dorms, first aid was administered to Grace and Amy was taken to the Infirmary to provide details about the incident.

In the cyclone of activity that followed, the paramedics were called, Grace was whisked to the hospital and all evidence at the scene was rendered invisible.

Grace would live. It was over.

But for Amy, something new had just begun.

* * * *

Dear Diary,

Of course they made me process after Grace's suicide attempt. Everyone was so sure that I would be traumatized. I guess I should have been.

But I wasn't.

It was so weird. It was like the whole thing happened in slow motion. I had all the time in the world to think about what to do — what to say. And I knew that I knew what to say. I was so sure of myself and calm. I even surprised myself. I had no doubt she would drop the blade if I just said so. I never doubted it for a second.

There, in that hallway, I had this vision. I saw me in the shower from so long ago — hopeless — a helpless little girl letting my

195

mommy undress me. And then, like I was out of my body hanging out on the ceiling, I saw me there, on the floor holding Grace, knowing what to do, just knowing. I wasn't the one being held anymore – I was the one holding.

Ms. Prudy wanted me to talk and talk about it so she could "help me through it". But I didn't need her. That was the amazing thing. I didn't need her.

One of my biggest fears in leaving this place was that I wouldn't have Prudy or Mr. Adams to prop me up and support me. But this thing made me realize I really don't need them to do that for me. I have their voices in my head. More importantly, I have MY voice in my head. And, judging from the incident in the hall – it's a good voice.

Who'd have thought, a year ago, that screw-up Amy would turn into hero Amy? But I did. Oh, not the kind of hero everyone is calling me. I don't leap tall buildings in a single bound. But I did step up when it counted.

And I do face the impossible and stand firm. I do try when other people would give up. That's who I am now. And it ain't half bad.

Love,

Amy

Epilogue

Ms. Pearl had taken Amy, Mia and several other girls out shopping to find graduation dresses. A local children's choir would be coming to sing and a parent who owned his own photography studio had offered to take pictures of each girl receiving her certificate and Climbing the Cs trophy. In honor of the ceremony, the kitchen staff had laid out deli meats, bread, a veggie plate and cookies. It was to be a big deal.

Mom and Dad had driven in for the ceremony. Even Lizzie had taken off from college so she could come along.

The kids were singing their last notes and the principal had stepped to the podium. Amy's heart was fluttering in her chest and her hands were pearled with perspiration as she waited behind the screen for her name to be called.

"Amy Miles!" announced the principal. "Since coming to Green Acres, Amy Miles has maintained a 3.0 grade point average. She has participated in both dance and outdoor activities, is part of the ASB, is a peer counselor and recently served as chair of our chemical dependency support group. Amy intends to return home to complete her senior year of high school and then move on to college, where she plans to become a counselor for troubled teens. Let's have a nice hand for Amy Miles."

As she stepped off the stage, Amy had to smile to herself. That was dramatically different from the 'drug-addicted, shoplifting, self-abusive screw-up' introduction she might have expected a year ago. Amy scanned the room of students and parents. People stood around in their best clothes, balancing plates of sandwiches and munching on cookies. Students introduced their parents to staff and friends. Everyone was laughing and sharing—acting like they were normal people.

Of course, no one in the room was normal. Not the students, not their parents, not the staff. Mental illness did that to people...and to all the people around them. But the certificate in her hand didn't lie. She had achieved something. She could achieve things. Ordinary things. Maybe even extraordinary things.

"So, my daughter," her mom said, putting her hand on Amy's shoulder. "Here's the sixty-four-thousand-dollar question. Who are you?"

From behind Amy's mom, Ms. Prudy's ears pricked up and she turned around to face Mrs. Miles and Amy. Wiping a cookie crumb from her lips, she added, "That's right, Amy. I'd like to hear the answer to that question. What do you say now?"

Amy smiled. Nothing had changed. Mom could be dogged about what she wanted. But somehow, it was okay. In fact, even though she hadn't thought about that question in some time, she was glad they were asking it now.

Amy paused for a moment to collect her thoughts. Then it hit her.

"I'm a diamond," she said.

Her mother twisted the ring on her finger and lifted her eyebrow. "Oh?"

"No, no, Mom. Not the shiny, polished, tamed diamond. That's not what I mean. I'm Mr. Adams' diamond."

"Did I hear my name?" Mr. Adams stepped up to the group, carrying a wrapped package in one hand and a glass of punch in the other.

"Remember what you said that day in class? That's me. I took all the sludge and muck that was my life and then used the pressure-cooker of my mental illness to force it into something of worth. But I'm not that slick, polished abomination," Amy said pointing to her mom's stone. "Oops," Amy corrected, noting her mother's raised eyebrow as she brushed her hand over her ring. "No offense, Mom."

"None taken."

"Instead, I'm one of those hot, raw, just ejected diamonds straight out of the volcano. Strong, unbreakable...and naturally beautiful!" Amy said, flipping her hair back for dramatic flair.

Her small audience chuckled appreciatively at Amy's joke as, one by one, she looked at the faces of the people who had changed her life — the people who had helped her turn from sludge to stone.

"Yes, dear," offered her mom. "That was the answer I was looking for."

"And here's this, Amy." Mr. Adams handed Amy the wrapped package in his hand. Amy immediately began to tear the paper to reveal the CD teacher's manual inside. "Keep this as a promise to your future. You have the talents and skills to change lives — keep this to remind you of all you have to offer."

Amy reached over and hugged Mr. Adams, then turned and embraced Ms. Prudy. Her mom went to shake hands with the two of them, froze, hand extended, then reached out and hugged them. Dad followed and soon everyone was hugging everyone.

"Amy?" Mom said as she brushed away a tear and reached to touch her daughter's back. "Are you about ready to go, honey?"

"We're eager to get you home," added her dad, as Amy caught his wink. Then, turning to Mr. Adams and Ms. Prudy, he said, "I think you've had her long enough — she's ours now."

"Take care of our girl," Mr. Adams said, patting Amy's shoulder.

Her bag was just outside the door, lined up with the other departing girls' suitcases. The girls had all said their goodbyes privately, before the graduation guests arrived. Amy had disengaged from Ms. Prudy and Mr. Adams and had said goodbye to Ms. Pearl. There really was no one left.

"Yeah, sure," Amy said. "Let's go."

Slowly, they snaked their way through the room one last time. Amy was just about to the door when Grace walked in, her arm and neck still heavily bandaged.

"Yo, girl," said Grace, grabbing Amy's arm.

"Just a minute, Mom," Amy said as Grace blocked her way.

Then Grace reached over and gave Amy a long, hard hug. "I'm waiting till the pain passes. But if it takes too long, I'll be comin' to find ya."

Amy smiled and let her hand brush along Grace's arm as they released their hold. "You do that."

"Let's go," she said, turning back to her family. And as her dad grabbed the bags, Amy pushed open the big glass doors and stepped out into the brilliance of the day.

Knowledge Is Power

Mental illness is common —

25% of people eighteen years and older have a diagnosable mental disorder. That's approximately 57.7 million people in any one year in the United States.

6% of the population, or one in seventeen adults, have a serious mental illness such as bipolar disorder or schizophrenia.

21% of nine- to seventeen-year-olds have a diagnosable mental or addictive disorder.

Mental illness can be devastating —

50% of people who will suffer lifetime mental illness begin having difficulties by age fourteen.

Suicide is the third leading cause of death in fifteen- to twenty-four-year olds. 90% of people who commit suicide have an underlying mental illness.

50% of teenagers with mental illness will drop out of school.

Mental illness is treatable and treatment can change lives —

Early identification and intervention can reduce long-term disabilities.

Treatment can be highly effective, especially if started early. Treatment can prevent loss of critical developmental years and reduce later difficulties and suffering.

Early identification and treatment also reduces delinquency, violence and crime.

Some of the most gifted people of all time have succeeded despite mental illness.

All statistics are from the National Alliance on Mental Illness (NAMI) —

www.nami.org/Learn-More/Mental-Health-By-the-Numbers
www.namica.org/resources/mental-illness/mental-illness-facts.

Resources

If you've been affected by any of the issues raised in *The Edge of Brilliance*, the following organizations may be able to provide help and advice —

Mind Charity — http://mind.org.uk

NHS — http://www.nhs.uk/Conditions/Bipolar-disorder/Pages/Prevention.aspx

International Bipolar Foundation — www.ibpf.org.

NAMI — *National Alliance on Mental Illness* — www.nami.org.
1-800-950-6264 M–F from ten a.m. to six p.m. EST
1-800-273-8255. This number is available twenty-four-seven.

Narcotics Anonymous — To find your nearest local meeting go to www.na.org

National Runaway Safeline — 1800RUNAWAY.

More books from
Finch Books

Broken by bullying, Tabitha volunteers and finds just what she needs to mend her life.

Like the colorful strokes of her brush, love changes the canvas of their lives.

Be careful who you keep secrets with, especially in picture-perfect Cherry Grove, a place where average isn't good enough, and nothing is what it seems.

Three years ago, Carson's sister ran away. Now he's found her — on a porn site.

About the Author

Susan Traugh

Susan Traugh is an award-winning author, wife and mother of three young adult children. For a decade she has been writing how-to guides for teens transitioning into adulthood, but when mental illness ravaged the life of one of her children, this book was born. Happily, both the book and the child have found their voice and their way.

Susan Traugh loves to hear from readers. You can find contact information, website details and an author profile page at https://www.finch-books.com/